Tomorrow a
and Tomorrow

MW00790494

Vikas Sharma
D.Lit.

www.diamondbook.in

All rights are reserved. No part of this publication may be reproduced, stored in a retrieval system or transmitted in any form or by any means, electronic, mechanical, photocopying, recording or otherwise, without the prior permission of the copyright holder.

© Author

Publisher : **Diamond Pocket Books (P) Ltd.**
X-30, Okhla Industrial Area, Phase-II
New Delhi-110020
Phone : 011-40712200
E-mail : sales@dpb.in
Website : www.dpb.in
Edition : 2023

Tomorrow and Tomorrow and Tomorrow (Novel)
Author - *Vikas Sharma*

All characters in this book are fictitious, and any resemblance to real persons, living or dead, is coincidental.

Where the ideas of parent and produce,
Purified thoughts and endless very varied forms,
Merge in the Real one; where the existence ends
Of such conception as 'within', 'without'—
The wind of modification being stilled—
That Hari I worship, the suppression
Of movements of the mind. Shiva I hail!

—**Swami Vivekananda**

1

Town Panipat started having industrial growth due to the trade of blankets, bedsheets, carpets etc. and the weavers could earn their bread with hard labour. As a lot of hospitals were constructed in major towns of the country, woollen blankets were in great demand. In hotels too quite a large number of tourists preferred blanket to quilt and the traders made money. Some of them concentrated on the production of carpets and exported them to U.S.A., U.K., Canada, Australia and a few Muslim countries. Cotton thread of various numbers was brought here from the thread mills of Malerkotla, Ludhiana, Baddi etc. and cotton bedsheets and towels were woven with the same. Demand of cotton bedsheets inspired the weavers to produce Jacquard cotton carpet, unique in itself and attractive in design and colour.

As there was work even for every poor person-male or female, there were no beggars in the town. Due to their health, the people depended upon jersey cows and consumed a lot of milk, yogurt and lassi as part of their morning breakfast, along with two potato pancakes. Partition of India had awakened them and due to hard times just after this major tragedy they realized that life without education was really worthless. They observed that their educated fellow brothers easily settled in India and the uneducated ones had to struggle very hard for their living. As a result, the followers of Sanatan Dharma established S.D. College on the outer skirt of Panipat. The devotees of Swami Dayananda learnt a lesson from this incident and built Arya College just in front of bus stand. The Jains added Intermediate classes to their Jain High School situated in the middle of the town.

Muslim weavers were happy with their trade relations with the local merchants of cotton items and nobody thought of propagating any ism among the people. Surprisingly, the second Babri Masjid was standing neglected and numberless bats had settled there long ago. There was one care-taker of the mosque and the Muslims had no time to offer namaz here even once a day. Even the grave of Ibrahim Lodi just near Tehsil area was lying neglected as if Lodis didn't live in the town. Unfortunately, Panipat had been battle ground for three major wars, and a large Maratha temple had been built here as a symbol of Maratha strength. Otherwise the residents were pretty busy since morning till evening.

There are five Jain Temples in the old Panipat and three of them fail to draw the attention of even Jains. Hardly anybody bothers for them and no renovation work has been initiated there. Jain Temple in Jain Street, near Jain Dharamshala, is the desired place where most of the devotees offer prayers every morning and evening and take out a procession annually to show their strength and faith to all and sundry. Many Jain families are wholesale traders of wheat, gram, barley, peanut, cereals etc. as there are four trade centres for their sale and purchase. Agriculture is one of main professions of surrounding rural areas of the town. In 1975 NTPC was established by the government to solve the problem of shortage of electricity.

Sugar Mill of Panipat crushes the sugarcane of the farmers and gives jobs to more than three hundred people. The population of the town has increased to two lac people and the banking sector provides a lot of financial assistance to various traders. It was after 1965 that Model Town was developed here in a large area and a lot of bungalows can be seen here and at the same time one can see the gap between Haves and Have-Nots here too. Nearly fifty percent people had no money to construct decent houses here and hence survive in simple homes looking towards the bungalows of rich merchants.

My classmates had settled on their parental shops after the B.A. Final examinations were over. But alas! I had no pole to get support and my worthy Papa Mander Dass, a subordinate clerk in Tehsil asked me in the last week of April —

'What do you intend to do after B.A.?'

'Join M.A. English.'

'But then Panipat colleges impart education only up to B.A.?'

'Yes. This is a problem.'

'Why don't you go to Thaneshwar or Ambala and study there? I hope my brothers must help you.' My mother suggested.

'They don't have enough rooms for their own children. Villages don't have academic facilities for students. No. No. That's no place to study.' My father retaliated with a sneer.

My mother left the room and became busy with cooking food. The topic of post-graduate studies remained unsolved and Papa left for office after taking his lunchbox. My brother Ajoy (15) was not worried of his career through education and played hockey almost every evening. My sister Toshi (13) was pretty like my mother and fortunately good in English and Social Science. My second brother Yatindra (11) enjoyed studying mathematics and a bit of Science. My youngest sister Natashi (9) enjoyed dancing with her friends of angry moods.

My parents never thought of the terms — 'standard of living', classical music, rock music, shopping expedition, picnics, clubs, parties, kitty parties etc. Fortunately, my Papa didn't drink wine, so common in Panipat and hence he spent his whole salary for the maintenance of seven of us. My grandparents lived in Jind and rarely visited us. My uncle Pranav Bhushan was a primary school teacher and had the burden of six children — Vasant (18), Ritu (17), Kushal (15), Mani (13) and Niwas Preeti (11). In his free hours, my grandfather felt worried about eleven grandchildren though he could never ask his sons to use contraceptives to control birth rate — It was a pitiable situation in which he found himself. Being a retired teacher, he preferred to stay in his dirty house in Jind. In his room he taught basics of English and Mathematics to small village children and earned his bread and butter — nothing to spare for sons and their children.

Fortunately, Lala Manik Lal lived just in front of our small house and concentrated upon his business of food-grains. Due to lack of large amount of money, he had to feel satisfied with his small income from purchase and sale of rice, wheat, gram etc. But he had to look after Palli (12), Multani Mal (11), Rishabh (9), Lakshaya (7) and Mehar (5). His wife Mala loved all her five sons and neighbours often called her mother of five Pandavas. She thanked God that none of her sons was a Duryodhan or Dusshasan. But she possessed wonderful patience as her mother-in-law became widow in her youth and had peevish temperament. In spite of Mala's best efforts and devotion to family, the worthy mother-in-law found fault in her work — either the salt in dal was little or more, vegetables had no taste cooked by her, tea had no sugar or extra sweet etc. At times Mala wanted to watch a movie but alas! widow known as Ammaji in the Jain Street was not prepared to look after her five grandchildren in Mala's absence though she loved all of them from the depth of heart. Grandsons were obedient to Amma ji and often ignored the dictates of Mala. One or the other slept in Amma's lap, not with Mala.

In the Tehsil office Papa had to work pretty hard from 10 A.M. to 7 P.M. Often he got some tips of fifty rupees and he purchased fruits. My mother felt irritated. On so many occasions she had instructed Papa to save some money for the marriage of two daughters — 'control your tongue and save something for their marriage.' But my father ignored her sincere advice and continued enjoying seasonal fruits. Now Amma ji advised my mother to save money for the marriage, and poor mom, knew her limitations as Papa detested any curtain lecture. Once my father told Amma ji — 'Bhabhi ji, I've two sons first and they're to arrange for the marriage of their sisters. How can a person arrange any marriage if he saves just a thousand rupees per year? Amma ji felt hurt with this argument.

Then Amma ji noticed that I started imitating Papa in matters of clothes. This added fuel to fire as if our paradise had fallen on earth. As a matter of fact, Papa had no luxuries to enjoy and wanted to feel a bit free in the present. Past had no value for him as my uncle had sold our share of land too for family affairs. As there was a big gap between Papa and uncle, the latter regarded the elder almost as his mentor. The land sold had no value — Done is done. The future was uncertain and yet Papa was planning for the education of five children. What else could be done in Panipat?

Since Lala Manik Lal's cashier was devilish and arrogant, the master had to be under the thumb of his subordinate. Quite often wrong figures were given to Lala Manik Lal and he had to adjust for lack of courage, physical strength and support of administration. But his cashier Ravi had guts to earn profits with the money of Manik Lal. All this continued for more than seven years. As expected the children of Manik Lal also grew up with time. Amma expected that all her five grandsons would be the best grain merchants of Panipat and no attention had been paid to their higher education. As a result, the eldest Palli passed B. Com. in second division. The second one Multani Mal became active in gambling and appeared in B.A. as a private student from a village college. Rishabh wanted to establish a factory and didn't bother about the poor situation of father.

Since Manik's sister Shobha got no child, she was allowed to adopt Lakshaya at an early stage. Brother Manik and his wife misjudged the financial resources of Shobha and expected bright future of Lakshaya in that family. Somehow Mehar developed interest in share market as his friend Nemi was expert in this growing trade. Irony of situation was that Ammaji observed all confusion and darkness in our family feeling sure that my sisters would die unmarried and we three brothers would prove to be worthless guys. On the contrary, Papa failed to expect any bright future for Manik Lal's five sons.

◼

2

It was daily routine of Mander Dass to visit Shiva's temple in the evening and count the beads 108 time reciting 'Namah Shivay'. On Tuesday he bought a coconut and asked me — 'Pritesh, accompany me to Shiva temple now.'

'O.K. Papa.' I replied and followed him to offer the prayer in the temple. I had the poem of Basavanna (translated by A.K. Ramanujan) in the temple after having offered the coconut :

The rich
Will make temples for Siva
What shall I,
a poor man,
do?
My legs are pillars,
the body the shrine,
the head a cupola
of gold.
Listen, O Lord of the meeting rivers,
things standing shall fall,
but the moving above shall stay ever.

I didn't know — the Lord listened my prayer or not? I didn't know — What would be my fate after the result of examination would be declared? After getting the Prasad from the priest I returned home with Papa and found him lost in grief. My parents wished me good luck though had no means to help me. Next morning my mother asked me — 'Pritesh, how did Vivekananda get the goal of his life? What about Lal Bahadur Shastri who had to swim in the river to reach his school? Don't you think the time has come for you to cross the ocean?'

'Yes Mom.' The result may be out any day.'

At the same time, there was a knocking at the door and I opened the door. To my dismay my classmates Yukti (18) and Dipali (17) were standing there. Dipali hugged me first and said — 'Congrats. You got first division in B.A.'

'What about you both?' I asked as I hugged Yukti.'

'Well, I just secured second division but Dipali got first.'

'Congrats to both of you. Don't lose heart Yukti as you can improve your division with improvement exam. Nothing to worry. Come in please.'

My Mom welcomed them though she had some knowledge of Yukti, the daughter of our family physician Dr. H. Singh. She sent Ajoy to the market to bring sweets to celebrate the event. Now Yukti asked me — 'What to do next yaar?'

Before I could speak I looked at my Mom and noticed that she felt hurt with the use of 'yaar' for me. Yet she asked Dipali — 'What do you intend to study next and where?'

'We both wish to join M.A. English but alas! There are no M.A. classes in three colleges of Panipat.'

Yukti asked my Mom — 'Where can I have a glass of water, auntie ji?'

'Don't worry. I'll bring for you.' Mom replied.

As Mom left for kitchen Yukti took my hand in her hand and said — 'Look Pritesh, we'll study at one place come what may. Keep it in mind as you can't turn down my plan.'

'That is O.K. Yukti. But I can't afford to go out of Panipat for higher education.' I lamented.

'My maternal uncle is Professor of Political Science in G.G. Singh University, Amritsar. I wish to join that university. You can accompany me without any problem.'

'No. Yaar, that is too far away. Expenses of central university, boarding and lodging and books are beyond my means. Sorry Yaar.' I said.

'Then, idiot, do you intend to sit idle on the bank of a river and wait for the favourable wind to blow so that you may move with the time? No way.' Yukti asserted.

'He can probably join S.D. College Ambala if my brothers agree.' My Mom told Yukti.

'Ambala? I doubt if the college has popular faculty members in English there?' Yukti almost turned down my Mom's proposal though the latter didn't know the exact meaning of popular faculty in S.D. College.'

As Ajoy brought the sweets, my mother left for the kitchen and Yukti finally told me — 'I won't join G.G. Singh University for your sake. I'll hire a flat in Ambala and you can share the same there. You needn't bother for any expenses. It will be a loan for you yaar.'

'Really. Is this offer for me too?' Dipali asked her. Yukti kissed her cheeks and said — 'Whyn't darling? That makes no difference. After all, I don't wish to get bored living in the hostel these days as the mess is topsy-turvy there. You know the scandals boys create for hostel girls. In the flat the maid prepares good food to our liking and Papa'll arrange a maid from Panipat itself. From Ambala we can visit Panipat as and when we like. Is it settled Pritesh?'

'Almost.'

'Why not definitely yaar? After all, Ambala is your choice?'

'That's all true. But there is a gap between the cup and the lip.'

'Look Pritesh. I am not asking your hand for marriage. Just I am planning for P.G. studies in Ambala.'

'Don't be serious as my Papa will take the final decision. At times he is quite fussy and adamant. Wait for a day or two and then we hopefully may join S.D. College, Ambala.

Both of them left after taking tea and sweets. I knew the gap that existed between me and my friends like Yukti, Dipali and Naini. Yukti's parents used to earn a lot of money from their nursing home and her mother Anuradha was M.S. and hence known in the town as the best surgeon. I had accompanied her to Ambala, Kurukshetra, Karnal, Jind, Sonipat etc. to take part in the seminars, debates and quiz contests. She needed company and security and I needed somebody to pay for travelling expenses. She had studied in Sharma Convent School since childhood with Dipali and Naini. Kamala Nain (18) was known as the best player of basketball and tennis and I had no interest in these games. Often I watched the rich guys playing tennis in the Downtown Club and hoped — Someday I too would play like them.

Last winter I was with Yukti in Shimla to attend a national seminar. We were the only students from under-graduate classes to present papers in the annual conference. The topic — *Validity of Novels With Political Purpose* — had been explained to us by Mr. Sharma of Panipat. After getting his books and guidance I prepared my paper on *Gandhism As Portrayed By R.K. Narayan, Mulk Raj Anand and V.S. Naipaul.* Yukti asserted that novels with political consciousness soon lose their significance as theories change with the change of times. Both had our arguments and the listeners admired our efforts. Rewards and prizes are not normally given to the speakers in the conference and yet the V.C. of Himachal University presented us *Advanced Learner's Dictionary* to boost our morale and we felt delighted with the intellectual atmosphere of a conference.

In the evening Yukti enjoyed champagne with her friends Dipali, Naini and Kamala Nain and I met Dr. Dahiya, former H.O.D. and Dean of Punjab University in his room. I took a risk and knocked at the door. As I was allowed to enter, I touched his legs and was blessed. He asked me — 'What do you want?'

'Sir, I wish to join M.A. English but my parents can't afford the expenses of my education.'

'O.K. No problem. I know Dr. Prem Prakash of Ambala and he'll manage everything as he did Ph.D. under my supervision. But then you've to behave decently there and concentrate only upon your studies. Library of S.D. College is pretty rich and hostel is there only for boys.' Then he gave me his visiting card and wrote two words for Dr. Prem Prakash on its back 'Help him'.

There was no limit to my joy when I had the blessings and promise of help from Dr. Dahiya. After I had left his room I met these girls strolling on the campus of the university and Yukti asked me — 'Where did you go? We were eager to join you for fun. After all, we are out of Panipat and can mix up freely here.'

'I had gone to meet Dr. Dahiya, a well-known scholar of Haryana. He has promised to help me for further studies.' I told them.

'That's great. This news must be celebrated yaar. You get a sort of passport to enter the world of intellect, the habitation of goddess Saraswati. Pritesh, come to my room and before we go for dinner, we can have some coffee and snacks.' Yukti proposed with mischief in her eyes and her friends thought they understood her intentions well. But, ironically, I could feel what she had in her mind. Just I hinted with my hand towards pocket — 'Look, we have dinner soon in the dining hall. Then we enjoy walking for half an hour and depart to our rooms for rest.' I told her frankly but she felt hurt as she failed to blackmail me emotionally.

'O.K. we meet in the dining hall after an hour.' She left with a sneer.

I tried to come out of self-gratification and thought of my Dharma to myself, to my parents, my studies, my job, competitions and above all the nation. Somehow my Papa and teachers had created my interest in the books of Vivekananda, R.N. Tagore, Bertrand Russell, Dr. Radhakrishnan, M.K. Gandhi and J.L. Nehru. From Vivekananda I had learnt the meaning of perception of life. From R.N. Tagore I had learnt the concept of self-enlightenment. Bertrand Russell's book on *Western Thought* taught me the theory — 'March ahead on the path of truth even if you are alone.' Dr. Radhakrishnan's book *Crisis of Faith* convinced me that I was supposed to march forward in spite of prevailing corruption and chaos. Gandhi ji's *The story of My Experiments With Truth* made me realize — If he could succeed in South Africa, why could I not get the aim in India? J.L. Nehru's book *The Discovery of India* created my interest in Indian culture and civilization.

Now I asked myself — 'How to overcome the demand of the slaves of consumerism? How to march ahead while surviving in the midst of rich girls like Yukti and Dipali? How to devote more time to studies? How to get rid of my childhood memories as they were full of sorrow and pity? How to judge the gap between right knowledge and worthless intelligence? How to be a real Man as G.B. Shaw asserted in the play *Man And Superman*? How to escape from the vanities and frivolities that I couldn't afford? And how to protect myself from the worthless pretensions of love?'

As I was growing young, I felt conscious of my passions and obsessions. But then the career could not be made without life of self-control and self-discipline. Jain Dharamshala was at a stone's throw from my home and I often listened the sermons of saints of all sects who delivered lectures there on soul, righteousness, mercy, fortitude, pure personality, self-knowledge etc. and these sermons were meaningful for me. I made a promise to myself to remember and practice the word 'Awareness'.

3

D_{r.} Sunny Thakur (44) was a learned Professor of Political Science in Arya College and enjoyed teaching the political theories of Plato, Aristotle, St. Augustine, J.J. Rousseau, Hobbes, Locke, Montesquieu, Karl Marx, Bentham, Mill etc. In spite of her command on Hindi language she aspired to be a novelist of English. Even after studying the theory of novel from the books of Arnold Kettle, Ralph Fox, E.M. Forster etc., she failed to develop her theme *Queen Isabella : The Witch*. She had torn more than forty pages and yet failed to develop the character of cunning Isabella. Even the exposition of the theme seemed difficult to her. Yet she didn't give up her efforts and wrote a few pages on the character of wicked Younger Mortimer who was equally opposed to Gaveston and King Edward II.

Dr. Sunny knew that Kamala Nain too was interested in writing novels. One day she asked her — 'How do you develop the plot so easily? I'm told that you have written two novels against British Imperialism with reference to Non-cooperation Movement and the Civil-disobedience Movement. Are you writing the third novel these days?'

'Yes Madam, I catch hold the ideas that come to my mind. After that select the particular idea to develop in a novel. Then I decide the method either first person narration or third person narration. Since language is no problem due to my convent education, I go on writing, developing the characters and laying emphasis upon conflicts between various forces. Please remember that conflict between two forces, people, nations, sections of society, members of a family, friends etc. is most necessary to develop the theme.'

Still Dr. Sunny failed to develop the conflict between Gaveston and Queen Isabella. Then she couldn't paint conflict between young Prince Edward III and Queen Isabella. She had spent more than a year and yet found herself at the stage where she had begun. Her husband realized her agony and advised her to give up writing the novel and try to write a book of political thoughts of various thinkers. That way she would make money and get popularity too. But then obsession is not given up easily by the artist — skilled or unskilled and he/she continues to create panic till it is fulfilled.

On the contrary, Kamala Nain had written her fourth novel on 14th century England with special reference to Black Death, Peasant's Revolt and the Renaissance and gave it the title *Awakening*. Then she wrote a novel on the life of Queen Elizabeth I with emphasis to new literary developments and the birth of republicanism and entitled it *Queen & The People*.

After studying the history of Industrial Revolution (1830-1950), the Information Revolution and the Bolshevik Revolution she started writing the next novel *Victoria III* and exposed the dark side of growing materialism, capitalism, culture, confusion, economic disparity, exploitation of poor nations by the developed nations, evils of colonialism etc. In this novel she had so far described the network of Victoria, the daughter of an U.S. industrialist, in India, Afghanistan, Pakistan, Indonesia, Bhutan and Nepal. In these countries she established her spinning mills and sold the yarn to Japan, Germany, Taiwan, Vietnam etc. She established Real Estate business in Noida, Gurugram, Bangalore, Chandigarh, Chennai, Mumbai, Lucknow and got one lac apartments constructed with a net profit of more than twenty percent. She knew — How was loan provided as loans were borrowed from Indian banks in the name of Victoria Towers. Then she invested one crore dollars in Auto sector and launched Victoria Electric car in India. On the pattern of Amazon and Flipkart she conducted home delivery business with victorian friends.

This novel confirmed Kamala Nain's understanding of eco-political and industrial world. Victoria became a capitalist of new era and Kamala Nain developed her character on the basis of Trump's economic activities in India and other Asian countries. In this novel she described the conflict between the manager of the units and the labourers. Cause of conflict was not economic exploitation as the workers were well-paid. The leaders tried their best to create racial differences telling the workers that British merchants will control Indian business again. They quoted the example of Sultan Jahangir who allowed a few British traders to have trade relations with India. Ultimately, the British traders captured Indian States with the help of money, dirty politics, racial discrimination, military force etc. and overpowered India with the help of East India Company.

Kamala Nain was a staunch realist and a supporter of humanitarianism. She asserted that Indian merchants were rich enough to establish every sort of Indian industry if they desired. Secondly, she found no shortage of many raw materials here for the production of essential goods. Thirdly, she pointed out that Indians were equally intelligent and let them stay in India after getting higher education with tax payer's money. That way she pointed out the conflict between Indian government and the Indian intellectuals who migrated to other countries for better jobs.

When I read the first five chapters of her manuscript in Ambala, I realized that the novel *Victoria III* was growing on the pattern of V.S. Naipaul's *An Enigma on Arrival.*

Kamala Nain felt happy with the material development of India after Independence and didn't feel disgusted with the British involvement in Indian economic affairs. When I talked to her about her hatred for British Victoria's approach she just replied — 'Indian clothes are well known for their quality all over the world. And then the Indian tailors can stitch good shirts, trousers, t-shirt, suits, etc. Same is the case with leather and steel goods. Why not to encourage only Indian goods to create jobs for our country men? One Lee shirt costs fifteen hundred rupees and you pay six hundred for Indian shirt. What a difference!'

Yukti, Dipali, Naini and Kamala Nain had joined self-finance Lala Lajpat Rai Centre For Post-graduate Studies And Research as the students could join M. Phil. just after passing M.A. and the topic of dissertation of M. Phil. could be developed for Ph.D. degree. But then the annual fees of one student was nearly three lac rupees per annum including boarding and lodging charges. Naini told me that hostel rooms had A.C. facility in summer season and study rooms and the library. I said to myself — Kabir, Surdas, Tulsidas etc. never thought of A.C. facilities and yet composed sublime poems. These girls visited their parents on each Sunday and I met parents once a month. There were five papers to be prepared and in each paper six authors were prescribed for detailed studies. Apart from this the whole section was divided into five literary societies such as Addison Society, Milton Society, Shakespearean Society, Henry Fielding Society and Dickensonians. Each student was to present at least one paper once a month and the marks for the same were added with annual mark-sheet.

Paper reading sessions were presided by students only and the supervision of faculty was vigilant. No indiscipline, no leg pulling of the paper reader and no useless questions! Dr. Sharma and Dr. Prem Prakash had been told by the principal to maintain the standard of teaching as the faculty was in competition with S.D. College. If any student was creative, his poem, prose-piece or short story was listened and then comments were asked for encouraging him/her. Positive approach was adopted and to my pleasure the library was pretty rich. Quite often Dipali and Yukti requested me for particular books. Yukti had spent twenty five thousand rupees for taking M.A. notes of Dr. Singh from Panipat. When I studied them, I found them bogus and planned to prepare my own notes with the help of British and American critics as many books published by Cambridge University Press and Oxford University Press were available in the open-shelf system.

To my surprise more than 40% students took education as a luxury as most of them hailed from rich families. Nearly 20% students were pretty serious and remained dedicated listeners in the lecture halls. They wanted to achieve their goal and a few were interested in I.A.S. and I.P.S. competitions.

4

Parents give birth to children and often choose their subjects for higher studies and yet fail to be the managers of their fate. Each child male or female has his/her own fate line. My brother Ajoy enjoyed the company of Kamala Nain's brother Hari Haran even outside the hockey play-field. Once Hari Haran was sitting on his jewellery shop and Ajoy gossiped there as usual. By chance a Naga Baba came there and asked Ajoy for a cup of tea. Ajoy thought for the friction of a second — to serve the Baba or to ignore his demand and the Baba told him — 'Boy, you have ten rupees in your left pocket. Pay rupees five out of it for my tea.'

Ajoy was shocked to hear this as he really possessed ten rupees given to him by Mom — five rupees for buying vegetables and five rupees as his monthly pocket money. He took a chance and served tea to Baba and touched his feet for blessings. After taking tea Naga Baba told him — 'Boy, your time has come to start a business of your own. By next month you'll be a rich man and then I'll visit you to get a woollen blanket.'

'O.K. Baba ji.' and Ajoy again touched his feet and Baba left.

That evening Panipat Trade Union had called a meeting of traders of the town to raise their voice against Tax policies of the government and Ajoy was requested by Hari Haran to join it just for fun. When Hari Haran was discussing deals with another friend, Vikrant asked Ajoy — 'What is your business in Panipat? Who are you as I have never seen you in the meetings before?'

Ajoy gave him his introduction and told him — 'I had come just for company's sake.'

Vikrant asked him further — 'Would you like to join my business of jewellery?'

'Sir, I don't have a penny to join jewellery trade.'

'That is why I am asking you to join me. Do as you are asked — nothing more, nothing else.' Vikrant said with confidence.

'O.K. I'll reach your shop tomorrow at 10 A.M. and see — how I can serve you?'

'Fine. Gentle man.' Vikrant left him with a smile.

Ajoy felt restless as he couldn't understand — Why did Vikrant need a penniless boy? What can he do on jewellery shop? What'll be his monthly pay? Will he be treated just as a servant? What about the permission of his Papa? What about his college attendance? Will he tell a lie to parents? Lost in all such unwanted questions he fell asleep.

Next morning he took a hasty bath and reached Shiva's temple and offered prayer —

'O Lord of the world
Known as preserver of all beings,
The source of health and wealth,
Mother and father of human race,
Beautiful with the moon on thy head,
Safe in spite of a snake around thy neck,
Help me in my job ...'

He had plucked two roses from the garden of his Jain Intermediate College and offered the same before Lord Shiva and counted the rosary beads 108 times 'Om Namah Shivay' and finally reached home to eat paranthas prepared by his mom. She noticed a change in his daily routine and yet kept mum. Then he reached the shop with a lot of doubts in his mind — 'Why has he offered me the job? What will he pay me in lieu of my studies? Will I succeed in this job? How'll I recognize the difference between metal and gold? How will I calculate the quantity of alloy mixed with particular ornaments?'

All his doubts appeared useless as Vikrant asked him to stand by his side and offer flowers before the silver statues of Maa Luxmi and God Shiva. After that he asked him to sit by his side, not to stand as a servant behind the chairs to watch the activities of the customers lest they should steal any item. Customers came, some of them bought a few ornaments and he was asked by Vikrant to count the cash money as received from the buyers. The very first day he could open the cash box of Vikrant with full confidence. It was totally beyond his understanding as his integrity was accepted by his employer, unknown to him till yesterday.

Vikrant (37) didn't doubt the conduct of Ajoy as Hari Haran had explained his simple and innocent nature to him last night. In the afternoon he was asked to have lunch with him. After lunch he was asked — 'Do you wear coat with the monogram?'

'It is lying useless in shelf.' Ajoy replied.

'No problem. Go home on the bike and bring back the monogram. I am sure you have your college identity card with your photo pasted and signed by the principal.'

'Yes that I have.'

'Bring that also for identification purpose.'

After seeing the monogram with Ajoy, Vikrant asked his cashier to bring the family tailor to the shop. The tailor took his measurement for coat, pant and shirt and was asked to collect the clothes from M/s Ahuja Cloth House. This too was astonishing for Ajoy but then he failed to gather courage to raise any question — Maybe this was all a part of the game of life.

In the evening he was given five hundred rupees to buy things of his liking and a packet of sweets by Vikrant — 'At least have a good beginning as my partner. Feel happy and jovial whatever be the situation. Don't appear dull and morose in public. Remember good things happen when your approach is positive. Bad things do happen with pessimists as they have no trust in Lord Shiva.'

My mother failed to understand — Why did Ajoy stop going the college? What made him join some business? How could a pauper be the partner of a jeweller? No. there must be some foul play somewhere. Due to excessive load of work and the state auditors being in the tehsil, Mander Dass had no time to look into this family matter. Moreover, he knew that Ajoy was the least interested in studies — Let him mind his business and let me concentrate upon other four children. Moreover, he often felt my absence in the family. I planned to visit Panipat after 5th September and that too for four hours.

Then packets of denomination of a thousand rupees were sealed in his coat pockets and five patches were stitched in the pockets of his pant. Thirty five packets were put in an ordinary old bag and he was given two hockey sticks specially prepared for this project. His ticket was booked by the Frontier Mail reaching Mumbai next day by 11 A.M. He was to stay in Nina Hotel room no. 305 and Vikrant asked him not to talk much with the strangers, and if inquired the purpose of his journey, to tell a lie that he is representing Haryana in All India Hockey Tournament to be held in Bombay. If his team wins, players will go to Goa for final match.

Willy-nilly mother wished Ajoy good luck in his venture. As instructed he remained silent most of the time. By chance he carried *As You Like It*, romantic-comedy by William Shakespeare. So far he had neglected this book. But then he struggled hard to understand the theme, the characters of Orlando, Oliver, Rosalind, Celia, Jaques, Senior Duke, Junior Duke etc. as he pretended to be brilliant student who wasted no time even outside home. Now he studied half of the book and with the help of paraphrase on right side of the text, he could follow 60% of the text. It was no problem to understand the character sketches and he realized that he should have prepared the book earlier. Due to his long silence as traveller he felt that he could enjoy other books of class 12th if he studied them — All books are not humbug anyway and he decided in his mind to devote four hours daily to his studies after this Mumbai adventure.

Evening tea and dinner were pretty nice as he had never enjoyed any such food. To his surprise a few fellow passengers enjoyed hard drinks in the compartment. Music was heard from the smart phone. But then he was in the world of uncertainties and didn't know — What'll happen next? He saw a dream in his sleep and started sweating as he failed to reach the examination hall and his father thrashed him badly for wasting one year of his academic year. His mother tried to protect him but could not. He felt pain in his back as cane of Papa had hit him badly. After a few seconds he got a jerk as one compartment was added to the train in Ratlam. He found that 'fancy' had cheated him as usual.

As instructed by Vikrant, Ajoy hired a taxi for Nina Hotel and moved towards room no. 304. After taking coffee he took a little rest and then enjoyed shower bath for the first time. He felt delighted to see that there were two big and two small towels inside the wash room. European seat was also new to him as he was habitual of using service latrine. For room service he rang to the reception and got lunch served in the room. So far he had enjoyed lunch prepared by his Mom — one dal and a few chapatis. Today he could order for things of his taste and hence ordered for tomato soup and new vegetables, apple salad etc. He couldn't eat as much as he had ordered. Yet he didn't bother for the wastage of food items and asked the waiter to preserve kheer in the fridge. Today he wanted to taste frozen kheer. Ice-cream cup was delicious and he took ice-cream twice.

After an hour there was a knock at the door and he said — 'Come in.'

One gentleman dressed in dark blue suit appeared and uttered — 'VIK.'

And Ajoy replied — 'RANT.'

Then the Stranger gave him a hundred rupees note with number 375477 and Ajoy confirmed it. Then Ajoy offered him note of fifty rupees No. 708806 and the Stranger accepted him as his friend and shook hands. The Stranger and Ajoy got confirmed with this and then the former took his one hockey stick and told him to wait for next morning.

After the departure of the Stranger, Ajoy got no mental rest as he had never dealt with any kind of business agent so far. It was his first experience in life and yet he had no option. Of course, he was not afraid of the opponent as he had faced many opponents on the play field — players who put stick in his legs, players who threatened him for making goals etc. The defeated hockey team members often became violent due to face saving. His parents were fed up with such violent activities and had advised him to play basketball or football or kabaddi. But then Ajoy was a growing boy with strength in his body and undemanding child in the family. For his only hobby of playing hockey he had never demanded any rupees as hockey and balls were regularly issued by the college. He had to skip the birthday party of his classmates as he could never dream of offering snack and coffee to them — Birthday function was not meant for the sons of poor parents. He consoled himself but didn't blame his Papa for ignoring his birthday too.

Ajoy felt a little sad as he failed to come out of the hotel to enjoy sight seeing, loitering on the sea-beach, shopping one item for each family member, meeting the film actor/actress if possible, playing badminton, seeing the Gateway of India etc. because he carried thirty lac cash money. What fun! He was out of Mumbai though. Leaving money in the hotel room was pretty risky as any damn thing could happen. He found himself the slave of money and a prisoner like a parrot in his cage. No limit to his desperation, lonely as he felt! How does a serious patient of diabetes suffer when physician bans all sweets for him?

Neither he had offended anybody nor anybody had harmed him and yet he was tense as if he was a prisoner. Out of desperateness he asked the waiter to buy a copy of *The Bhagwadgita* for him. After half an hour he started reading the same and concentrated upon 'detachment', 'renunciation', 'liberation', 'duty of man' etc. He asked himself — How is kingly glory superior to life contentment that his father had in Panipat? What did Babar get after defeating Ibrahim Lodi in 1526? Was Babar not to be blamed for killing a lot of Lodi soldiers? How could war be justified? Why did Duryodhana not adjust with Pandavas in the large palace of Hastinapur? And what did he get after insulting Draupadi after manipulating success in the game of chess?

Ajoy offered prayer before the brass statue of Lord Krishna at the gate of the hotel but demanded nothing from Him and dropped one note of hundred rupees in the donation box.

As he returned to the room, he found the same man at the gate of his room with two hockey sticks. The man bolted the door and took thirty lacs cash from him and instructed him — 'Look Ajoy. One stick belongs to Vikrant and A alphabet is mentioned in the middle. And the second stick is divided in two parts — the lower the 'gold rod' giving you ten lac rupees cash and that'll be your share and no need to reveal to Vikrant. Rods contain worth twenty lacs and they also belong to you as payment of your risk taking power. Is everything clear to you?'

'Yes it is.' Ajoy replied.

The Stranger added — 'I hope your first visit will be highly rewarding. In case you visit Mumbai on alternate dates, you can contact me on phone too. My number is 9999000005 ...'

'I reply when I get back.' Ajoy replied and offered him coffee. Then he offered him laddus as prepared by mom. He promised to help him in every situation. He felt sad for not having him as his guest as many intelligence officers watched his bungalow round the clock.

Ajoy's temperament as a hockey player created no tension on his face and he put the bag and sticks on the top of sleeping berth. He had normal dinner, coffee etc. and reached Panipat, not by the scheduled train but by the next train after two hours. First, he left the second hockey, half-fitted at home, took tea and put the money in the book shelf and reached the shop of Vikrant with the hockey.

Vikrant was already upset as Ajoy had switched off his phone in Mumbai itself. Moreover, he was not used to phone service by then. He asked Vikrant to take out gold bars from the manipulated hockey stick (2007). It was this year that gold prices had started shooting up by one thousand rupees for ten grams gold. The cashier and the concerned technician calculated

the price of gold rods and told him just after fifteen minutes —
'All is O.K. Sir.'

'Fine. Bring one bar costing ten lacs.' Vikrant told the cashier.

Then he handed over that to Ajoy as a reward of his service and said — 'I have earned fifteen lacs more with this successful operation of yours. You can enjoy ten lacs as my gift. Did you have any problem in your journey — Panipat to Mumbai and back?'

'No sir. My problem was loneliness because I couldn't move out of hotel as I carried cash. On way back I had sticks and that too was a risky affair. Hopelessly I couldn't enjoy Mumbai visit.' He told him plainly.

'Don't worry. Sometime I'll send you there with your wife for honeymoon. Then you'll be able to enjoy.'

5

Within next three weeks Vikrant sent Ajoy to Mumbai three times and hockey sticks and hockey player's monogram saved his skin. My brother didn't sell the gold bars that he got from Vikrant as gift. Secondly, the bars in the upper part of his hockey were supposed to be pretty in the small bullion market. Same dealing and same people and the same commodity and above all Ajoy's grace under pressure made him a crorepati and Papa knew nothing what had happened in his own home. Mom doubted the intentions of Ajoy but as usual kept mum.

But Vikrant's wife Sunaina played a trick with her husband when he revealed the secret that gold price has shot up to twenty thousand per ten grams and he was one of the richest people of Panipat. Instead of feeling gay and jubilant she sadly lamented — 'What's the wisdom in having large amount of money if our two children can't get the best education in Panipat.'

As Vikrant was not even a graduate, he thought that Panipat's convent schools were nice as he had been taught in the municipal school up to 5th and then studied in Jain High School up to 10th and then joined his Papa's jewellery business. His father arranged his marriage with the daughter of Delhi's bullion merchant without understanding the needs and aspirants of Delhi girls. Here Sunaina couldn't join late evening parties as her younger sister Gati did in New Delhi. On phone the sisters talked of the gap between the tehsil and the capital. Gati's kids studied in International School of Dwarka and she was free for almost three hours after sending children to school. Maidservant prepared the lunch and the servant delivered tiffin to her husband, a wholesale cloth merchant on Lawrence Road. They enjoyed Pizza frequently in the Pizza Hut and Bengali sweets was there to cater to their taste. The driver took her to Palika Bazar and Khan Market and she had bought a lot of imported goods for her family. Sunaina aspired for a car, which could not be managed in this ancestral house near tehsil.

Quite often Vikrant also aspired for the modern Delhi life that Gati enjoyed but then suppressed his ambitions. All of a sudden all his gold assets made him a man of crores and he planned to buy a shop in the upcoming mall of Dwarka. The property agent made it possible for him to get 20'×20' shop in Dwarka for one crore rupees. As the registration formalities were completed, the carpenters were asked to furnish it and Vikrant made a proposal to Ajoy to buy his shop. Ajoy felt delighted with this offer but expressed unwillingness so as to get it on cheap rate. He replied — 'You know sir, that I got what you gave me. Amount of twenty lacs is not enough to run jewellery business.'

'You don't worry for the money. Buy my shop for twenty lacs, get registration work done and pay me later on in instalments.'

'What'll be the amount of instalment by the way sir?'

'Well, pay me twenty thousand rupees per month without any interest. If you can spare ten lacs now, it'll ease my problem. If not, doesn't matter. I'll manage.'

Vikrant left the shop quite often and bought three BHK for one crore and twenty lac rupees in Dwarka. He bought Honda City car costing more than eight lac rupees to please his wife and children. Furniture was bought from Karol Bagh to feel modern and advanced and dinner was taken on the dining table. Somehow he failed to relish the food that the maidservant prepared and frankly told Sunaina — 'Hell with this rubbish food. Why can't you prepare four chapatis for me as you did in Panipat. I feel sorry for shifting here.'

This was a clear indication for her to mend her ways. She had spent more than ten lacs upon clothes and he had no idea about that. Soon the kids told him — 'Mom is not at home when we come back from school. Maid doesn't prepare nice food.'

He realized the fact that Gati had poisoned the whole affair but had the patience to take proper action as he knew — How to nip in the bud? Sunaina started complaining of pain in abdomen as she wanted him to join her for morning walk. But that was the time to help children Bittoo and Kittoo for the school. Yet he took her to the newly built extra modern hospital of Dwarka and all the reports were normal.

With every tomorrow Vikrant expected that Sunaina would mend her ways and look after the children. On the recommendation of college principal he requested Sushma ji (26) to help the children in studies specially science. Yet Sunaina remained free, careless of home and husband. Soon he realized that this so called modernism was hell of affair and planned to return to Panipat. But then children and Sunaina resisted against this approach of Vikrant and turned down the proposal. On the contrary, second car was demanded by the kids for free movement to school, birthday parties and picnics. He was told that extra curricular activities were part of the project reports on the historical buildings of Delhi and nearby areas. Visit to the Red Fort, Gandhi Samadhi, Lodi Road, Humayun Tomb, Museum, Parliament, Raisina Hill, Qutab Minar etc. was essential. Since Vikrant had been taught with Hindi-medium, he found himself lost in the world of English medium people.

Income from Dwarka shop was rather minor and every tomorrow created new hopes in him. He sent advertisements of his shop and allowed 20% discount on all diamond ornaments. Sunaina was not prepared to share his financial problems as she fulfilled her ambitions with credit card. All the four members had their mobile sets and home was regarded as a place where they took rest at night and food if they felt interested. He found to his surprise that each family known to his wife and children celebrated birthday of each child, of parents and of course wedding anniversary. He knew that his worthy wife had become a real Memsahib and thought of her rights rather than duties. There was no one to check her and unchecked liberty was something that she had aspired for.

Often she slept with Gati's husband Sakal Tadapi and felt delighted. Gati also flirted with Pratyaksh, husband of her friend and children weren't prepared to work hard for examination. Schools needed money and hence the students were promoted to the next class on the basis of their non-academic activities. Tour to distant place was part of the curriculum and Vikrant had to finance the same. Smart ladies of kitty parties enjoyed outgoing once a month and that too for two days as they got bored with the dull routine of home. It was just a 'change' for the better — A rolling stone gathers no moss.

When Vikrant's father was seriously ill, he advised him — 'Look Vikrant, maybe the time has come for me to depart. Take care of farming and never sell ancestral land of village Johi. That'll prove to be the greatest support in times of adversity. Secondly, be watchful in daily expense as these young men turn diamonds into pennies and people like me turned pennies into gold coins. Thirdly, I'll be leaving you in a sound position as no bills are to be paid. Lastly, cut your coat according to your cloth.' And he breathed his last.

Today Vikrant felt very lonely on the shop as the number of customers was scanty. Yet his intuition gave him two positive replies — Income from interest is enough to meet the expenses of family and income from farming was still his saving. With future the demand for diamond jewellery will improve and he too would create reserve funds for his children. Quite often he respected the days when he wished to be sole controller of shop affairs and failed to control his wife and look after his children. But then he had no power to revive the past. He stood before the photo picture of his father and confessed his innocent feelings. In his dreams he found himself relaxing in the lap of his worthy mother who had died of cancer. He met his father in dreams and listened to his warning — Life may not give you a second opportunity. Sinking man rarely gets a hand of support.

'After taking breakfast he asked himself — Was he really sinking down the pool of life? Will his income never improve? Will he not succeed as a jeweller in Dwarka? Will the prices of gold remain stable? Will his gold assets give him more money? On phone his friend Hari Haran advised him — 'Look yaar, value of gold may not improve but then rest assured, it won't disappoint you at all. There are rumours that gold price will soon go up by ten thousand rupees per ten gram. This is a temporary phase as there is in every trade. Personally I hope to regain profits with time — if not in three-four months, a year after the price is bound to go up. Why to feel worried when things are out of our control.'

And this friendly advice consoled him a lot and he continued to see the interest results and listened to the opinions of experts of bullion market.

Vikrant visited Panipat on each Sunday so as to manage the farming affairs and felt free after 2 P.M. Then he rejoined Ajoy on the shop and inquired about the progress the latter had made. He suggested the latter to invest his money @ of 2 percent interest in his Dwarka shop but the former ignored the plea saying — 'I don't have enough to invest elsewhere.'

My Papa's colleague Triveni Babu asked him sweets for being the owner of Vikrant Jewellery shop and gave him the documents of registration. He felt stunned — How did Ajoy manage five lac rupees? Who could lend him such a large money? That made him restless. He told all this to Mom and she had a mild reaction of fear and joy — Ajoy had told her about the prediction of Naga Baba and she saw a new blanket in the almirah of Ajoy to be gifted to Baba ji. She thought — But then the results would be unbearable if Ajoy gambled/stole things, enjoyed speculation trade etc.

Sometime she felt that Ajoy was bad smelling when he returned home late. He had started smoking cigarettes and nothing could be definitely said about him. Moreover, Papa failed to understand how could the shop costing more than twenty lacs could be bought just for five lacs by Ajoy. But the question was — Who'll bell the cat?

That night my mom took the risk and directly asked him — 'How could you manage to buy the jewellery shop Ajoy?' Without waiting for his answer she gave him the certified copy of registration.

'Mom, I told you about the prediction of Naga Baba. This is the miracle of his prophecy.'

'But Baba never gave you five lacs. Moreover, your Papa told me that the shop costs at least twenty lacs. How did you get it for just for five lacs?'

'Perhaps Papa ji didn't read the details of registration. More money has got to be paid to Vikrant in regular monthly instalments.'

'Who'll support you to run jewellery shop?' Mom probed further.

'Vikrant Sir, Who else?'

'Can I make a request to you?'

Now Ajoy had tears in his eyes and left the bed and touched her feet saying — 'Why do you doubt your son? I am Ajoy, your second son. I am no thief or a cheat. Just I have been offered an opportunity to make money and it is a matter of chance that gold price shot up from four thousand to twenty thousand per ten gram.

'Mom, your son is a man of two crores. We can arrange for the education and marriage of sisters. No worry for future of sisters.'

'And where is the money?' She asked with anxiety.

He showed her the money lying at the back of books in the almirah though dust had gathered on the books.

◪

6

Money comes slowly and regularly in small quantity but bumper gain is rare and my Mom knew it well. Papa told her that Ajoy bought the shop in his own name whereas he could have saved 2% registration charges if he had bought in mother's name. As a matter of fact, Vikrant got all the registration papers prepared protecting his personal interests and Ajoy failed to understand mixed Hindi, English and Urdu words used in the documents. His satisfaction was beyond limits as he owned jewellery shop. Due to his respect for Vikrant, he didn't get the board repainted in his own name. But then Vikrant advised him to contact the lawyer and Excise Officer to run the business. He tried his level best to trace the difference between metal and gold, diamond and jerkin etc. and appointed an expert for this purpose for fifteen thousand rupees per month.

After six visits to Mumbai he was a man of nearly three crores. But the Stranger in Nina Hotel Mumbai had recently become independent wholesale dealer of gold and told his real name to Ajoy — 'I am Tonny Raja, wholesale dealer of gold biscuits. If you don't have time to come to Mumbai, the goods can be delivered in Panipat on 5% extra amount. Take your decision and tell me on my cell.'

'Fine. Thank you.'

Ajoy didn't discuss this with anyone and asked Tonny Raja for fifteen percent commission if purchase is in bulk i.e., fifty biscuits at a time. Tonny agreed immediately and Ajoy started selling gold biscuits to the jewellers of Haryana and Punjab towns.

He was hardly seventeen years of age and Papa thought — son had no worldly wisdom. When Vikrant visited Panipat, he brought two whisky bottles with him and stayed in his ancestral home and the maid prepared salad and dinner and then left. Molly was invited for physical pleasure as she was famous for gentle massage. After 5 P.M. Vikrant asked Molly to join him, massage his body and then had fun with her. Somehow he asked Ajoy — 'Did you ever enjoy massage with Thai oils?'

'What is that?'

'You'll enjoy it today after 6 P.M.'

As instructed Molly had most minimum clothes on her body and gave a nice massage to Ajoy. He felt excited and failed to control his passion. As he caught her hand and moved forward to kiss her, she replied — 'Every service has got to be paid darling.'

'Come on yaar. Don't worry.'

He kissed her bosom, cheeks, neck, thighs and then wanted to proceed further. She warned him again — 'Every service needs a payment.'

'Come on darling. Let me make love.'

Inexperienced as was, he could not enter her properly and she guided him as she too felt equally passionate. She expected to be paid at least five thousand for two hours but Ajoy had never dealt with call girls earlier and expected payment of one thousand rupees maximum.

Ajoy felt shy, not Molly. She told him how to have sexual pleasure with a woman in different manners. It was his first chance to be with a naked young girl and had not expected it to be so pleasant, rewarding, delightful and satisfying. After foreplay he entered her and she asked him for strokes. He failed to relish when she mildly cried out of pain. Innocently he asked her — 'Does it hurt you Molly?'

'Yes, it does. But then it is a pleasant hitting affair. Go on darling.'

'Ajoy enjoyed pressing her hips and breasts and played with her nipples. As he tried to squeeze her breast, she warned him — 'Play with them, don't squeeze.'

'O.K. fine.'

After a pleasant trip Ajoy felt happy with his first sexual adventure. Both of them exchanged their phone numbers and she asked him to book a room in Titania Hotel as and when he desired to have fun. But he lost his temper when she demanded — 'Give me five thousand rupees my Raja for today.'

'Are you kidding Molly?'

'No. You have enjoyed for more than two hours. Vikrant Sir pays me ten thousand rupees for six hours. No bargain. No call girl has such breasts, cheeks and hips as I have. Maybe you get Aids from them.'

Immediately Ajoy paid her five thousand rupees and got himself checked for Aids in Taneja Derma Centre.

Papa and Mom had no idea about these moral lapses of Ajoy but some other jewellers knew the weaknesses of Vikrant — A depraved son of a worthy father upon whom Fate had so far been favourable.

On 20th January Mom asked Ajoy — 'How do you plan for your sisters, their education and marriage?'

'As you guide me. Nothing to worry.'

'Will you follow my advice, my son?'

'Yes. Why not? Speak whatever you've in your mind.'

'Ajoy, deposit ten lac rupees in each sister's account for their marriage, though it is too early to ask for this favour.'

'Has Papa asked you for all this?'

'No. Not at all. As usual he remains busy in his tehsil work. Often I find him dull and dormant. These days he doesn't speak much as he used to.'

Ajoy left the bed, opened the almirah and showed her three bank passbooks — ten lacs each in the names of Toshi, Yatindra and Natashi and in these joint accounts, he himself was the second account holder. Mother had been nominated as nominee. He further told her that two apartments have been booked in Akash Apartments costing forty lacs each and probably all of them will be shifting there after six months or so.

Papa could not dare to interfere in the private life of Ajoy as the latter never needed former's advice. The son had earned the amount that Papa won't be able to make in the whole career. If he felt some affection for Ajoy, he sat on his shop for fifteen minutes or so. Ajoy offered him tea and samosa and burfi every time he was there. When he left, he was handed over a packet of sweets for the family. But there was total confusion and uneasiness in Papa's mind and Mom failed to analyze the dark side of this business.

Every month Ajoy gave two thousand rupees to Toshi and Natashi and paid extra if they needed books. Tuition money was paid without grudges. They were allowed to buy necessary clothes from Ahuja Cloth House where Vikrant still had credit account. Monthly gifts were sent to Excise Officer, I.T.O. and the S.O. Kotwali.

Ajoy didn't have any self-control and was controlled by his lust for sexual pleasure. Parties continued in the hotel room almost daily costing a lot to him. Whenever Molly had period, she brought Sally with her. He waited for 6 P.M. as and when he was free. He had become the victim of honey trap because he had no knowledge of time management and husbandry, never calculating what he earned and how much he spent. Thoughtlessly he enjoyed sex and drinks and Papa and Mom failed to poke their nose in his affairs.

Papa could not dare to seek any guidance from anybody as he could realize that Ajoy had become pretty rich due to smuggling of gold and fortunately the sudden rise in gold prices was unprecedented. Papa reached Lord Shiva's temple with Mom and stood before the Lord and goddess Parvati and offered the prayer — 'Oh Lord, you are the symbol of truth, beauty, wisdom and righteousness, the beginning and end of everything. Kindly help me to get peace of mind and guide this idiot son to mend his ways or else he would return to his original self. Let him be wise and prudent and maintain balance between income and expenses. It is with your grace that money had come to him and maybe problems of marriage of two daughters get solved. But then he is to be reduced to zero if he continues to waste money like this.

'Om Namah Shivay, Om Namah Shivay, Om Namah Shivay!' Both of them left the temple with a heavy heart as if a tragedy happened that very night in the family.

All this routine of Ajoy continued for more than three months. As ill luck would have it, customers from Jind, Karnal and Ambala told lies that they had not taken second delivery of gold biscuits. Since Ajoy could not file any complaint, he had to tolerate the loss. But then misfortunes never come alone and he met an accident against the car on Panipat-Karnal Highway and along with Molly his bike fell into the ditch 7' deep on the left side of the road. Somehow, Molly could save herself and informed the police with the phone of Ajoy about the accident and left him unprotected.

Police Sub-inspector and two constables carried him to government hospital and got him admitted. At about 1 P.M. Papa received the call about Ajoy's fracture in right hand and collar bone and that created panic in the family. Papa, Mom and Yatindra reached the hospital with money so as to take care of unwise Ajoy. But then the worst was not yet over. The surgeon and the physician had taken his X-rays and E.C.G. and asked Papa to take Ajoy to Ganga Ram Hospital New Delhi for further treatment and operation.

Papa was already a heart-broken fellow and expected tragedy in life due to unethical trade practices of Ajoy. But then next day the cardiac surgeon of Ganga Ram Hospital told him — 'Ajoy's two heart arteries are almost blocked. With angiography we'll make further investigations. Fractures are not very serious and there is no danger to his life. Deposit four lac rupees at the counter soon.'

Mom was wise enough to carry two lac rupees to New Delhi and the same was immediately deposited at the counter. Papa found ATM card in the pocket of Ajoy and the latter a little conscious, revealed his code to him.

This is how Ajoy's treatment was done by the concerned physicians and surgeons. He was to be detained in hospital for at least three days for further investigations. His hand was plastered and the collar bone was operated. Sorbitrate tablet was given twice a day and Papa was asked — 'Should we go ahead with angioplasty of his arteries for putting two stents?'

'Please do what you deem proper.'

'Then buy stents from the chemist shop.'

Mom had to return to Panipat to take money from Ajoy's almirah. That way his operation got delayed for a day. As I was busy with studies, I was not even informed. Papa and Mom also had to suffer the results of his lust. Ajoy took the hand of Mom in his hand and felt sorry — 'Sorry Mom. Not to be repeated in future.'

'It is O.K. Relax as it is a question of heart.'

Physician instructed Ajoy not to touch alcohol in life as his lungs too were badly affected. My sisters lived alone in Panipat and offered prayers to God for the wellness of Ajoy.

Since Tonny Raja had no information of Ajoy's accident, he had bought thirty biscuits and needed payment. Finding the shop closed he made a phone call to Ajoy and then reached Ganga Ram Hospital. After expressing his sympathy he gave him the biscuits and asked him not to worry for payment. Since Raja was going to the Golden Temple of Amritsar, he asked Ajoy to manage the money within thirty hours otherwise his Man would collect the same after a week or so. In the ear of Ajoy he warned him — 'Don't trust the gold merchants and never sell gold on credit. Credit cuts the cords of friendship and brotherhood. My case is different since you are helpless. Take care. If somebody is playing foul, give me his name. Don't worry. I know how to get back the money from such debtors. Bye.' Then he left the hospital.

❒

7

Yukti, Naini and Kamala Nain had been blossoming regularly and I paid attention towards the smartness of Yukti as she played badminton in the hall of Mrs. Shraddha. Since I was a beginner in the game, she could defeat me easily. However, Mrs. Shraddha (30) noticed my agony and suggested certain tricks to improve my game. She played one game with me before Yukti joined us. It was Ambala club and Mrs. Shraddha was its owner after the death of her father. Mrs. Shraddha and her late husband Vinamra studied together in the Army School of Amritsar and came closer to each other. The father of Shraddha late captain Sri Ram had intimate relations with Major Krishna Kanta as both of them had their agriculture land in Alipur, Ambala. Captain Sri Ram built a luxurious house with three floors in Ambala and Shraddha lived here with her old mother Sarla, a patient of paralysis. Captain Sri Ram and Major Krishna Kant had died in the battle of Kargil and yet Shraddha was well-off. Her husband Vinamra died in a car accident just after three months of marriage. Due to her positive approach to life, she didn't surrender before cruel blows of fate and continued to read the lastest books to pass the time. Secondly, she visited her father's farm on alternate days though often wept standing in the verandah of farmhouse. She recollected her childhood when she had played various games with Vinamra. Often they quarrelled with each other as she felt cheated in points. There was a water pond near the tubewell and she still enjoyed swimming and playing with water. Quite often her tear mixed with tubewell water but there was none to console her. The guard and the gardener maintained the farmhouse and cultivation work was given to a reliable retired Subedar on contract.

Mother of Vinamra soon died after the death of her husband as she was a heart patient. The miserable young man was bidden final adieu by his loving wife with whom he had hoped to pass the whole of his life. Often fate plays one trick after another and Mrs. Shraddha had not hoped to be the owner of eight hundred bighas of land, cash money of her father and father-in-law plus pension of her husband.

Books were in abundance in her personal library as her father-in-law and husband were fond of reading books written by sublime authors. Taking inspiration from Robert Southey's poem *The Scholar* she spent much of her time in the library. In the evening she directed three-four guys for acting in the film because she had learnt the skills of theatre and creative writing.

She asked these guys to learn the plays of Christopher Marlowe, William Shakespeare, Henrik Ibsen, G.B. Shaw, Eugene O' Neill, Arthur Miller etc. Since she didn't charge any fees from these guys, they took it lightly. Often she felt that these guys were worthless — neither smart nor intelligent enough to earn their living with acting. Sometimes she could feel that they wanted to flirt with her emotions and each one took her to be his heroine. Naturally, she felt disgruntled due to their rubbish conduct and asked them not to visit her any more. Yet she took interest in playing badminton with Yukti, Naini and me. It was a real pleasure to enjoy coffee with her as served by her maidservant Dhania.

Being highly sensitive and extra emotional, I felt a little shy with Shraddha as she paid for everything. Quite often Yukti came forward to pay for shuttlecocks, but madam smiled and said — 'Don't worry. It is my hobby. I feel happy in your company. But don't defeat Pritesh regularly as he is a learner. Soon he'll learn playing good game and then ...'

'I'll wait for that time.' Yukti replied.

I just smiled as Madam often touched my hand to guide — 'How to serve? How to smash? How to cover the court? How to play to win with placing?' etc. Her touch created a thrill in my body, young as I was. Soon I started thinking of her beautiful figure and sympathized with her widowhood. She had all assets and was really super in every sense.

It was month of October and Yukti had left for Panipat with Naini and Kamala Nain. I stayed back in Ambala as I had to prepare some class notes. It was hell of a problem to carry books to Panipat. Secondly, I got used to my hostel facilities. But then the cook closed the hostel mess for five days.

As usual I reached Shraddha's house to enjoy badminton. Since Yukti didn't come, she played two games with me and made me win. While playing the games, I noticed the rise and fall of her breasts, her parted hair and her attractive well-built thighs. Today she noticed my eyes — What did they want? After I had won two games, she shook hands with me and kissed me on my cheek saying — 'Well played youngman. Had you concentrated on the game, you would have secured more points. Today I got defeated and hence your victory must be celebrated.'

We entered her drawing-room and she asked me to have a shower before enjoying party. I told her not to think of party as I had no clothes to change.

She promised — 'Why do you worry young man? You'll first have a shower, change the kit and then we gossip for a while. Is it O.K.?'

I couldn't say no to her proposal as her breasts and thighs were taking me out of my senses. I wished to kiss her in return but then hesitated lest she should get offended. I had a shower in the second washroom and imagined her nude body with my fancy. But the image was not ready to disappear. After the shower I felt somewhat romantic and dared to kiss her in the drawing-room finding her in new shorts and a small sleeveless shirt.

The table had two glasses, bottle of champagne, apples and dry fruits. As she filled my glass, I told her — 'I don't take wine.'

'But champagne is no wine. It is drunk on such occasion of victory and celebration. Are you not happy with your victory? Don't you like my company?'

'It's not so. But then ...'

But she had half-filled the glasses and said — 'Cheers. For the health of innocent Pritesh.'

She moved by my side and offered the glass to me. I had to imitate her to look advanced and polished in manners as she had turned out four guys for their rubbish conduct. I took the glass from her hand and tasted champagne. One cup soothed my body and I forget the tiredness of games. She took my left hand and put it on her thighs — 'I saw you observing my whole body today and that too passionately. Here I'm and you can kiss any part of my body. I'm unable to control my sensation.'

Now she opened two buttons of her shirt and took my hand there.

For the first time I was rubbing the boobs of young woman. She kissed me on my lips and neck and asked me to think of the union of Madeline and Porphyro in *The Eve of St. Agnes.* 'Accept me as your Madeline, my Porphyro. I have nothing else to offer to you accept my love. Don't deny the bliss of union of love.'

I hardly bothered for the second cup of champagne though I had heard high of it. There was none to disturb us and it was a nice party-celebration which had been purposely managed by her. I wanted to go to the hostel but she badly resisted — 'Your mess is closed for five days. Stay with me for this period and study the books four hours a day. It is after five months that I have the company of a nice guy. Please don't leave me incomplete and unsatisfied.'

Before dinner we finished the second glass of champagne and talked a bit on socio-political issues of the world. Since war had taken her father and father-in-law, she had no faith in the glory of war and like Bluntschli, hated war. She cursed the people who have no traffic sense and create unfortunate scenes on the roads for unwanted and unexpected accidents. I wiped her tears when she narrated the tragic episode of her husband's death.

After dinner she carried me to her bedroom which had been decorated with many rose-petals. Both of us enjoyed foreplay and made love freely thrice. I found her witty and cheerful like Louka. At about 2 A.M. she took me near the window and asked me to watch the moon in full bloom. She told me about S.T. Coleridge's Christabel who came out of her palace to enjoy the beauty of the moon and met ghost type lady Geraldine. Again and again she kissed me and wanted to be sure of my love for her.

In the morning she offered me tea and after that we moved towards her gym where she enjoyed a lot of exercises. The gym was fully equipped and she guided me how to enjoy various exercises to remain fit and fine. She noticed my eyes and found them watching her whole-self again and she proposed—'Perhaps you are eager for me as I am for you. We'll enjoy once again and then you'll study in my husband's study room for three hours. I'll offer prayers to Lord Krishna as usual. We meet again at 12 O'clock and plan for future.'

'O.K. Madam,' I said and thought that she might not have the needed books. To my surprise her library was pretty rich and I got books that I wanted. Morning breakfast was served to me in the study room. I studied John Donne's poems with forced concentration as my mind frequently thought of her physical charms. At last I wrote an answer on Charles Lamb's style so as to make use of the time and not appear to be a fool of love. And this came to be true when she met me for coffee. She asked me — 'Could you study in loneliness?'

'Yes. I could.'

'What did you study in the last three hours?' She asked with a smile on her lips.

'Well, I studied three love poems of John Donne. Then I revised a question on Charles Lamb.'

'Fine. Will you tell me the difference between knowledge and wisdom?' She eagerly asked.

'Well, I think people have knowledge after they have studied a lot of books. But there is wisdom that comes with experience and society of good friends.'

I replied with full self-reliance. And I added — 'Knowledge without wisdom is incomplete guide in life.'

'Great, Pritesh! What do you find in me knowledge or wisdom?' She cunningly asked and I was not prepared for such a direct question.

Still I replied — 'Perhaps time will reply this question to both of us.' I told her.

'Pretty clever. You have avoided my question but I'll ask it again sometime else.'

'O.K. Let me analyze your question for some more time.' I said.

Yet she didn't leave this topic and argued — 'Was it my wisdom to surrender my whole-self to you last night?' She asked.

'Well, you can better reply this question yourself as it was planned neither by you nor by me. It was outburst of our mutual passion for each other. Otherwise also, I take you to be a considerate and thoughtful young girl who would not take foolish steps come what may.' I tried to convince her with my kiss on her cheeks which she relished.

After lunch we gossiped in her drawing room and she asked the details of my family and just remarked :

'A long way to go. Pritesh. Really tough time to face regularly. But I can solve some of your problems if you trust me and also allow me to have full faith in you?'

For a moment I was taken aback and remained silent. She mildly proposed — 'Life is hell without love and money. Look at me, I have money but no love. How long to lead life of Lady of Shallot who was not allowed to enjoy the beautiful things of the world? How long to live alone with a patient of paralysis? Even in Ambala Club I feel restless as lustful men wish to flirt with me. Am I a vegetable or fruit to be bought by these so called refined people? Will you trust me now?'

She caught my hands firmly and kissed my cheeks. She put my hand on her boobs and said :

'I belong to you forever and forever if you can just trust my love and me as woman? I have never cheated anybody but fate has cheated me twice. Your problems will be taken care of by me. If you wish to be a professor, you'll get all facilities here.

I can take care of your family too as there are twelve rooms in this bungalow. There is no hurry if you wish to take time to decide your reply. No force to force your love for me. Is there?

There was a turmoil in my mind, a conflict between knowledge and wisdom. I told her frankly — 'Madam, give me some time to analyze the issue as there has been no planning in our game of love. Trust me as I don't have any money to offer you a ring as token of my love for you. I told her frankly and then she told me of Robert Browning who eloped with Elizabeth Barrett Browning to Italy and led a happy married life there. I recollected Browning's line — 'Who knows the world may end tonight!'

8

In the last summer vacations I felt tempted to study Dr. Har Dayal's famous book *Hints For Self-culture* and Karl Marx's *The Communist Manifesto*. Dr. Har Dayal awakened my interest in intellectual culture and asked the readers — you eat four-five times a day for physical growth but then — Do you study five times a day? I was not a book-worm as I didn't have the financial resources to buy the latest books written by new writers of 21st century. Due to my bad luck the University Grants Commission of New Delhi had stopped giving annual financial assistance to aided colleges after 2014 and hence there was no purchase of new books in my college too. Most of the Indian colleges had depended upon U.G.C. for annual financial assistance. But then I was helpless. Secondly, Indian rich students usually spent money on hobbies and mobile phones and not on books. I read a sentence on the jacket of book — A room without books is a body without soul. That way my house was soulless as new books could not be added to that. I knew the financial limitations of my Papa and hence didn't like to create any tension for him.

However, two lecturers of my college helped me get books issued from the college library in the months of April, May, June and July and I selected the books from there for my reading. Frankly speaking, I agreed with Har Dayal that real readers get joy in knowing from books. A lot of authors have written essays and books on the importance of books as they don't ask the readers their name, gender, caste, nationality and mostly create universalism in them. Writers creating racial prejudices become unpopular soon and authors as T.S. Eliot and V.S. Naipaul remain ever fresh due to their love for mankind as a whole.

In the essay *Poor Relations* Charles Lamb refers to this fact that books are above prejudices. Many critics go to the extent of asserting that propaganda literature is short-lived and does not appeal to all readers of future generation. According to I.A. Richards, a good book stands tests of time and place. After reading *Hints For Self-culture* I became extra conscious of the value of time as it was limited for everybody and the time wasted never returns. There were no short cuts for progress and I was to be a bread-earner for myself and a helping hand for my kind-hearted parents.

In most of the Indian families parents regularly ask their children to cut the time they spend in games and gossips. In my case my mother almost forced me to enjoy walking in the morning and evening so as to get fresh air. In a funny mood I often told her that there was no fresh air in Panipat due to new factories that have been recently established here and polluted the environment.

In the summer vacations my friend Sudeep asked me to join a cotton mill as a clerk. I felt a little tempted but my Papa asked me to think of further studies only as he could provide food and clothes (though very ordinary). I couldn't imagine buying jeans, T-Shirts of Monte Carlo and Lancer shoes as a pair of chappals was enough for me. Papa rightly told me (when he was in a peaceful mood) that 'education period is that of Sadhana — Think new ideas, move forward and don't repent for past follies.'

And Papa was right though he was not even a graduate. He joined tehsil as a clerk just after passing intermediate and since then had not been able to buy any woollen suit for himself. My mother had knit one pullover for every member of the family and that used to be our woollen luxury. Once Papa told me that body needed protection from cold weather and a modern suit does not give any warmth to the body and hence not needed. I often aspired for suit with a necktie but alas!

There was poverty in the family due to limited means of income but there was love among all seven of us. My parents never asked me to support them in their old age as Papa depended upon his pension and gratuity forgetting that he will have to spend large amount of money in the marriage of sisters.

Unfortunately, my uncle never encouraged me to study regularly and asked Papa to let me search a private job in Panipat itself. Amma ji as usual felt worried about the five of us.

While reading *The Communist Manifesto* I silently developed a dislike for the industrialists and exporters of Panipat. While going to the college I regularly observed the miseries of poor labourers who could not afford for medicines in old age. Often they failed to arrange money for the marriage of young daughters and let them continue working for carpet weavers. Jobs were not that rare in Panipat due to handloom and power-loom units but wages were disgusting. Then the formula of every merchant was — First come, first serve. Secondly, some merchants used muscle power too to manage the units. Single sentence — Exploitation explains the whole industrial scenario.

While reading Karl Marx I felt agitated as labourers had to work for more than ten hours a day. Secondly, the working conditions were unhealthy and tough. Very rare merchants provided two jeans and a jacket (very low quality) so that the labourers could protect themselves from cold weather. Sincere and dedicated labourers could manage jobs for the wives and growing children and they had no hope for bright future through education. Education was O.K. in convent schools and not government schools — All students didn't come to get education and every teacher didn't come to teach well. Even the money meant for mid-day meals was manipulated and labourers were worried of physical needs as they had no concept of intellectual needs. They hardly hoped for a new era in which the Proletariat will control the economic system of the state and the country. Quite often they offered prayers in the temples built by local landlords and industrialists and yet the labourers failed to accept that 'religion was an opium'. Even in slums and huts, one could see the paper pictures and clay statues of Lord Shiva, Lord Vishnu, Lord Rama and Lord Krishna but not that of goddess Saraswati.

One Sunday I asked an unknown labourer as the latter was cursing his fate — 'Do you know the name of Saraswati?' He replied — 'Maybe she is some film heroine.' That was direct indication of his intellectual penury. It was in 1840 that Karl Marx wrote *The Communist Manifesto* but even the new Marxists had not studied this *Bible* meant for the labourers. I just thought of irony of situation — Karl Marx led a miserable life to write the books in support of labourers. But alas! The latter had no knowledge about this superb philosopher, called a 'devil' by the capitalists and a 'Messiha' by labourers. In spite of being a Jew and a native German, he faced no language problem in London but his followers failed to illustrate his principle of

M

A

R

X

I

S

M

to his followers.

As a student of B.A., with keen interest in Economics, I reached the huts of labourers to prepare the budget of a labourer for my college project. Since I was seen there by one of tehsil colleagues of my father and he told my Papa about my interest in labour problems. Without my Marxist leanings I was labelled a hardcore Marxist by him and my father and the worthy mother set me right– 'It's pretty hard to look after the family these days. In case you get arrested as a Marxist here, I don't have the money to get you released on bail. Why don't you concentrate upon your studies? Tell me the name of the person who puts such silly ideas in your mind. Is knowledge going to make you go astray?'

My innocent mother felt non-plussed and failed to realize the error of judgment. I tried my best to convince Papa that budget preparation is just a part of my project. Now he said — 'I'll ask my office peon Ram Lal to come here. You can prepare budget with his help. He is already a poor fellow with six children. He too lives in slums if slums matter in the budget.'

I had to forget my interest in Marxism that day and promised Papa not to visit the slums of labourers. However, fifty percent labourers of Panipat had really tough time during dengue days. But a few wise and prudent industrialists gave fifty percent wages to their dedicated labourers and even supported their families through thick and thin. They knew that dengue will disappear one day and they are going to run their units in future as new business needed more money and new expertise which they didn't have. I realized the fact of the statement — Need makes us adjust with the patient crying for tooth-ache.

❒

9

Second day when I reached the dining table for lunch I found a sheet of paper before me with my name and its interpretation :

P — Prudent

R — Regular

I — Intelligent

T — Technical

E — Energetic

S — Smart

H — Honest

For moments I felt flattered and thanked Madam for the compliments. She just smiled and asked — 'Did you analyze yourself like this earlier?'

'Frankly speaking, never!'

'But in these last eighteen hours or so I have thought a lot about you as a person, as a friend, as a player, as a student, as an ambitious person, as a polite fellow, and ...'. She hesitated.

'And ... what else Madam?'

'And as a lover, a trusted partner and a deserving fellow standing on the threshold of new period in life. Remember Pritesh, opportunity knocks at your door only once.'

'Well, I wish to create new opportunities with my higher education and with the blessings of Lord Shiva, parents and friends like you, I hope to succeed. And success earned with fair means is really rewarding. I believe in simple living and high thinking.' I told her.

'Let me see the results of your high thinking. Thinking on classroom topics may not be that rewarding. Often the students with bookish knowledge fail to cross the bridge of life as uneducated swimmer succeeds against the horrible waves. Frankly, you haven't seen the complexities of this society where people struggle for existence and there is cut-throat competition on all the corners. You, being a beginner, will have to struggle hard for bread and butter. Realities, specially financial realities, shatter our nerves and force us to make compromises that we had never planned in our scheme of things.'

I noticed wrinkles on her forehead and her eyes were wet with tears. I knew that I had not referred to her past to find tears in her eyes and yet reached her chair to console her and patted her back saying — 'I don't have any intention to hurt you in any way. Sorry if you felt hurt.'

She took my hand in her hand and guided me to sit by her side. I told her — 'Desires make us dance badly for fulfilment. Decision inspires us to work hard for the goal and madam, hope is eternal and makes hell of heaven.'

She felt a little easy now and said — 'I have been trying to manage life with self-determination, courage and of course hope is my best friend. Now I offered the first morsel to her. She accepted the same and offered a morsel to me also out of sincerity to assure me of her love for me. But she remained silent for the whole time and I generally take food silently. After lunch she asked me — 'Are you free Pritesh? I wish to buy some clothes for myself. We come back after an hour or so?'

'Sure. I am free for two hours. Then I study for some time and after that enjoy badminton with my princess Madam.'

She left for her bedroom and I waited for her passionately. Somehow I felt myself restless as nothing was certain. Still I became conscious of my passion for her. It was not a film to come to an end after three hours. The theme had just begun in this bungalow and maybe she too was taking a big risky step with me. But then — What can't be cured must be endured. Moreover, I had nothing to lose so far.

She was dressed in almond colour silk saree with sleeveless blouse and appeared gorgeous and superb. Her small purse was also golden and the diamond necklace added to the beauty of her neck. As she came out of bedroom she asked me — 'How do I look Pritesh? Is everything alright?'

'You look a goddess and a Maharani in this silken saree. Nice to be smart and active.'

'Any other compliments?'

'Yes.'

I moved towards her and kissed her hand and then on her right check. As I felt erection in my penis, I wished to be with her in bed but that needed postponement as she was eager to go out and said — 'Let's go out otherwise we would get late.'

'But what is the hurry?' I asked.

'No time should be wasted. Since you have to study books after shopping, I wish we come back home by 3 P.M. Come along with me.'

'O.K. As you deem proper.'

It was my first time to be inside an A.C. car and she asked me to sit on the front seat by her side. On way to Mall she asked me — 'Are you not enthusiastic now?'

'Yes. I'm. It is a pleasure to be by your side. Sometimes we can enjoy a long drive in the moon light.' I suggested looking towards her.

'You'll make me crazy definitely.' She smiled and yet concentrated on driving.

It was a new surprise to be inside the Eve Mall as it was almost crowded with young people and children. Since she had been regular customer here, the man on the counter welcomed her and she needed no direction to reach the female section of garments. She preferred to buy two white jeans, two nighties, four bras, four panties, four sleeveless shirts and four kits for games' purpose. Then she took me to the male section of garments and repeated my sentence 'It is good Pritesh that you believe in simple living and high thinking. But your simplicity needs to be adjusted with 'high living' if you don't mind. Since we trust each other now, please buy some garments as gifts from your princess. Please don't dishearten me. If you don't buy clothes for yourself, I'll return my purchases too. Will you just oblige me?'

And she had my hand in her hand at this moment and took it to her lips to kiss. I was already passionate and hence kissed her on her cheeks.

Without showing distaste for new clothes I bought two blue jeans, two white jeans, two terricot pants and a white suit. Then I selected pair of socks for myself as she politely suggested — 'Pants without smart shirts?'

'Fine O.K.'

Then I bought six shirts, two pairs of Lancer shoes and four kits for badminton too. Ties had to be bought on her insistence. She was eager to buy more things for me but I forbade saying — 'Next time.'

After taking ice-cream from another counter, she paid the bill with her credit card and the attendant carried our things to the car. I found her happy as I had obeyed her command. Of course, I imagined — I would look a smart guy in these branded clothes. Let me sail with the flow of water and not ride the waves against the flow.

In the car I told her — 'I hope you are happy with this shopping?'

'Well, women are never fully contented with shopping. The more you buy, the more you wish to buy. Things are displayed in a nice and attractive manner by the interior designer. Ultimately eyes remain rich and hands often remain half-empty. Are you happy with your selection of clothes? I wish you look smart before every one. After all, we are rising above the feelings of mine and thine now.'

It was a meaningful sentence now, to make me think. True that she had surrendered her body to me but then I had to concentrate upon studies to become a college Professor and feel independent.'

I kept silent and she asked again — 'Are you sad Pritesh due to any thought? Did you want to buy other things too?' She asked with a wrinkle on her face.

I rubbed her hand saying — 'No. Whatever things have been gifted by you, will remain in my mind. This confirms your trust in me. I'm really delighted with you and additionally pleased with these gifts.' I told her.

❏

10

I put my packets on the dining table and she directly entered her bedroom to keep her purchases there. But she came out dressed in white jeans and white shirt and asked me — 'Does this suit me? Do I look smart in this dress too? It is after long time I am wearing white jeans with white shirt.'

I went close to her and kissed her cheeks saying — 'You look like a perfect cricketer in this dress.'

Then I pressed her boobs and she knew I was already passionate as my nostrils were producing warmth. She didn't resist and carried me to bedroom. Here I pressed her lips and boobs and she put her fingers in my hair and said — 'Only thing I expect from you is trust. I have led the life of a discarded widow in the last three months. Perhaps Yukti has been guided by Fate to introduce you to me. You came to play badminton only but you have conquered my emotions, feelings and obsessions. Nothing beyond your love dear Pritesh. You can share your problems with me any time and God willing they will be solved.'

I made love to her forgetting that I was supposed to study in another room. The study room had been cleaned by Dhania and a new comfortable chair and a table lamp had been put there. One double bed had already been lying there. The date was changed on the calendar and the wall clock gave the right time. She asked

Dhania to put my packets here as the old wooden almirah had been emptied. It had attached washroom which one of them used in emergency in the morning. But there was no tub for joint bath for which I felt eager.

She was all humble in bed and active too as she had experience of love-making. Then she had been loved by her husband and I was in an uncertain condition. Mine was a vehement passion for a young woman. After we had enjoyed love-making she left for her washroom and I followed her. She asked — 'Why didn't you knock at the door?'

'No question of mine and thine between you and me as you said in the car.'

'O.K.'

I took her hand to enter the tub and then we played for half an hour to our heart's content. She told me — 'House is full of pleasure and bliss with your arrival. It is pleasant rain in this desert. Please keep it up. When lovers are united, even gods are jealous. If you recollect, many gods disguised themselves as Nala when Damayanti was having her Swayamber. Since Damayanti had been taught to know the difference between a God and a human being, she could select Nala, the hero of her heart and garlanded him, much to the agony of gods. Secondly, it is said that human beings can get salvation with good deeds and

R
I
G
H
T

C
O
N
D
U
C
T

'I understand what you mean.' I told her and kissed her bosom to assure her of my trust. I said — 'I am no legendary hero with super-human powers and Kingly Palace. Frankly speaking, I depend upon you so far. You are the captain of my ship and can carry me in the direction you want.'

After coming out of the washroom she appeared all the more fresh. Now she asked me to change the clothes and try jeans and shirt to try the size. I appeared pretty smart now and had changed in her presence without any hesitation. She remarked :

'High living with high thinking now onwards.'

And she entered her storeroom and brought two diamond rings and an imported wrist watch. She asked me — 'Put your finger before me please.'

She pushed the ring in my finger and unexpectedly touched my legs — 'This is the symbol of my trust in you.'

Without waiting for a minute she gave me the second ring to be pushed in her finger. I took her hand in mine and then offered the nice female diamond ring in her finger and then kissed her hand. She then tied the watch on my wrist. She was damn pleased at this moment and embraced me.

She had ordered the maid to decorate the table in the third room and we reached there the next moment. The gardener had decorated it with various flowers and the maid had put snacks and champagne there. She filled the glasses saying — 'Cheers. For a happy married life with an unknown

S

T

R

A

N

G

E

R

who is to be my guide, mentor, friend and my Man.

I made her sip champagne from my glass. The door was already closed and hence I could enjoy kissing her boobs and hips. Slowly she removed my jeans and T-shirt and we were passionate enough to celebrate this first ceremony of our love. All of a sudden she said — 'Wait a moment.'

And then she took two gold chains from the pocket of her gown and offered one to me. She asked me to put the other one round her neck. Her chain had a diamond pendent and it touched her boobs — just in the middle of two boobs. I sarcastically said — 'This pendent will be a disturbing factor to me.'

'No. Not at all. I'll take care of it. This exchange of chains confirms further that we will ever

C

H

E

R

I

S

H

each other. Am I wrong in my guess?'

'No. Since you're sincere and frank, I admire your sense of integrity and sincerity. We begin this new journey with mutual trust.' Again we kissed each other.

It was 9 P.M. now and she asked the maid to lay the table for dinner. Important dish was that of milk-kheer, a ceremonial dish served to the members of bridegroom's family and prepared by the new bride. I didn't mind if kheer had been prepared by the maid for the occasion. At least courtesy was observed and after dinner we returned to the bedroom and were in the arms of each other.

She told me a few adventures of her N.C.C. period as she had been Under Officer in the district and quite active in shooting and driving. Due to her father's active life, she had been trained to appear smart, active, well-polished and well-dressed. She made me conscious indirectly that I was supposed to remain smart as I was the best companion in her life.

Next morning she had an early bath and then offered prayers to Gods in her Pooja room. I could hear the Bhajan she was reciting. I left the bed, shaved myself and put on the new dress and reached her Pooja room with flowers. She felt happy with my devotion to God — At least I was not an atheist as communists generally were.

After we had finished breakfast she took me to the drawing room and asked — 'Can I be frank with you regarding the aim of your life? What do you wish to achieve and how?' She abruptly asked.

'I wish to be a college professor after passing M.A.' I replied as my interview had begun.

'Fine. But then do you know the new conditions and qualifications for degree college job?'

'Is there any change in that?' I eagerly asked.

'Yes. After passing M.A. you have to join research under the supervision of an expert guide. Research work and viva-voce will take five to six years at least as I have enquired. Secondly, you have to clear National Eligibility Test with

M

E

R

I

T

as only 6% candidates are declared successful from the top rank. N.E.T. will require studies of two-three years. Then the result of N.E.T. and then the posting by the Higher Education Board of Haryana will take more than a year. Nobody can help you to get any result in a short time as you are aware of red-tapism in India.

I became totally nervous with this clear picture as put before me. I wished to be a college Professor. She came to my side and put her hand on my head and played with my hair with love. Realities are often unbearable and my house of cards had crumbled as I was not in a position to wait for five-six years for a job. I had overheard my parents when my mother offered him two gold bangles to sell for my education at Ambala.

As she realized my agony she tried to comfort me saying — 'Rome was not built in a day.'

And secondly — 'Work with love and don't expect thy reward' is the lesson of *The Gita*.

'Look Pritesh, you accepted that wisdom and prudence are superior to knowledge. Do you hear me?'

'Yes.'

'Then it is time for you to be prudent. I suggest two options for you if you think about them —'

'What are they?'

'First, you study for M.A. degree and you need one and a half years to finish P.G. studies. Then you join research for college Professorship.' She stopped.

'Your second option?' I eagerly asked her as I was enthralled with her prudent analysis of my academic career.

'Options can be many. But then hard work and planning are required for that. Are you ready to do that?' She asked.

'Yes. I don't have any other option.'

'Don't accept anything merely because your princess Madam is suggesting them.' She warned.

'No. I won't be emotional. But many jobs require a lot of money.'

'Yes. You have hit the right point. My second option is — We both start the business of blankets as people prefer to use blankets and not quilts. Their rooms and houses are small and it's hell of a problem to keep four-five cotton quilts.'

'H'm.'

'Question is — Do you wish to manufacture them or have their trading. To my mind manufacturing unit needs a lot of money. Secondly, labour problem is there. Thirdly, it'll take 2-3 years to establish our branded blankets. What do you suggest?'

'Well, trading of blankets seems to be best option. I have been a student of Economics and my Professor suggested — Think of both the sides of trade-profit as well as loss. What'll happen if we don't succeed for one reason or the other.' I asked her with a tense mood.

'No risk, no gain and secondly I'm in a position to take the risk of a few lacs due to my agriculture land income. You just make the plan for the ground floor rooms and we soon shift to first floor.' She reasonably suggested and smiled.

She added — 'Don't have any tension in trade because we have enough money for bread and butter. Think for a day more as you'll have a job of your own to make you feel you're employed. In case you still think of professor-ship, I can start a M.B.A. college in the building of my father-in-law from the next session. There you'll be boss and C.E.O. of college, much above Professor. Plan as job giver and not simply job-seeker. After all, we are one after the exchange of rings and this is the beginning of mutual trust. Is it O.K.? Do you feel pacified or not? I still have options if you don't like trading of blankets?' She looked at me with anxiety.

'No madam. Another option will be discussed if we fail to start this blanket trading. I'll prepare the project report to be cleared by C.A., the bank and the industry department. Om Namah Shivay.'

'Om Namah Shivay.' She repeated.

11

I felt as if I was totally free from the hostel life and forgot the full freedom that I had enjoyed there. Madam's company was the best source of my delight and I didn't remember my parents and the trio — Yukti, Naini and Kamala Nain. Of course, Yukti and Naini had visited my brother's jewellery shop to buy a pair of diamond ear-rings and informed him of the closure of hostel mess for five days. As a result, my mother was quite bothered about my food and didn't know that I was enjoying delicious food and champagne with Madam. We both played two games of badminton for two days and had party celebrations.

Third day Madam told me after taking breakfast — 'We may start blanket trade in the rooms of ground floor and shift our living on the first floor. What do you think?'

'Your plan is fine. But then the rooms have got to be renovated for trade purpose as they are basically meant for living. Secondly, I would suggest you to buy a few steel almirahs for keeping the stock of blankets and shawls the reason being that woollen clothes gather dust soon. These items have got to be saved from moth, pests and rats. Thirdly, an interior designer will suggest better in case we wish to have a sales counter too.'

'These are superb ideas. First, the four rooms are to be tiled with Kajaria Tiles. 5' walls have got to be tiled for grace. Glass windows and doors will be required. And of course the show cases have got to be installed. Two (2 Tons) A.C. will serve the purpose. Plus 10 LED light tubes will be required. Mattresses will be put in all the four rooms. How many steel almirahs will be required in the beginning?'

'Well 15-20 will serve the purpose. We'll need one almirah for records too. One computer operator, one computer and one printer will be required. Plus one price gun is needed.' I mildly suggested her.

'Fine. First, the contractor will prepare the floors of first two rooms and then the floors of first floor. After the first floor is completed we shift our bedroom, drawing room and kitchen upstairs. I plan to order for the installation of one lift so that the rooms on second floor may be utilized. There we can have a guest room, billiards table and squash.'

Then she looked towards me for further suggestion. But I had no suggestion to add as I had not yet seen these two floors. After all, I had my limits and I didn't wish to create any tension for her. Of course, I had no doubts about her vigour, zeal and enthusiasm for trading of blankets. Since the almirah manufacturer was known to her, she ordered him to send 15 steel heavy almirahs to keep the blankets safe.

After offering morning prayers I asked her to talk to family Pandit for an auspicious date for opening of the trade and also have Mahapuja of Lord Shiva and Lord Krishna. She okeyed the matter and asked the maid to bring Pandit ji next morning.

After having breakfast she told me to accompany her to the bank so that a saving bank account may be opened and credit card/A.T.M. facility may be obtained. Just I intervened — 'If you don't mind, we should go to Lord Shiva's temple this morning. Let's us have the blessings of the Lord today itself.'

'Fine idea. We leave home at 9 A.M., offer prayers in Shiva's temple, buy a mobile phone for you and then reach the bank. Right it seems?'

'Of course, right. After that?'

'After the bank work we proceed to Amritsar and then Ludhiana to see the market for trading and find out the possibilities in this trade. Is it O.K., Pritesh?'

'Yes Madam.'

I had forty five minutes at my disposal and I prepared a rough project of the trade. Maybe she asks for it soon. As I had sketched the rough plan, the maid asked me to see her. She felt pleased seeing the outlines of the project and the estimated cost was two crores — one crore for blankets, 20 lacs for shawls (male), 30 lacs for shawls (female), 30 lacs for lohis and two lacs for A.C. blankets. Since madam had made up her mind for one and a half crores, I said — 'Let us survey the markets and then finalize the numbers of items and the needed investment.'

'Right. That's the right course.' She replied and left for dressing up herself. I dressed myself well to look smart and then we left for the temple. Of course, she looked most gorgeous in white chiffon saree and backless blouse. I carried my college identity card, Aadhar number and photo.

Pandit ji welcomed her in the temple and blessed both of us without knowing our relationship. He was ready to come to her bungalow any time he was required and hence gave her his cell number. It was after a long time that I had visited any Shiva temple and she felt delighted to see my faith in God and His blessings. She said at the gate of temple — 'Well begun is half done.'

'Yes. Of course.' I replied.

She bought MI mobile for me as I had no particular choice. She gave her address for my identification and felt happy saying — 'Use it as and when you like. If we are away from each other, we can contact and chalk out the programme.'

'Thank you for this gift madam.' I said.

'Stop thanking for everything. Yet many things have got to be done to create self-reliance in you.' She said and made eyes at me.

In the Syndicate Bank she got fifty lac rupees transferred in my new S.B. account and I felt dazzled as I had never dreamt of such heavy amount. It was joint account and she was the second operator in either or survivor. Then she asked the manager to add my name in F.D. R.s of one crore rupees. She nominated me as the person to take care of her locker if something unfortunate happens. It was too much on her part and she had just asked not to be thankful again and again and I yet gathered moral courage to thank her for her trust in me.

The manager of the Bank ordered for glasses of juice and that gave a little relief in this scorching heat. But soon he asked her a real favour 'Madam, our bank building needs a bigger counter and more room for proper service of customers. There is room enough in front of your bungalow as my cashier told me and if you can oblige us it will be very kind of you.'

'Well, you've just asked me for the bank building. It needs some discussion and time. Hopefully something will be done. After all, Bank is a bank, a real necessity in this digital age. Bye. Thanks.' She told him and left the chair.

In the car she told me — 'You're a responsible man now. I don't think what else can be done to win your faith and trust. I have moved three steps towards you and now it is your turn to move towards me.'

She smiled before she could start the car. As the car had coloured glass, I moved towards her and kissed her cheeks and pressed her thighs. I simply said — 'I won't disappoint you in any way.'

'Remember your promises. O.K.?'

'Yes, O.K.'

❏

12

While coming out of the Bank I saw an elderly lady whose face resembled with that of my mother. Naturally I recollected my mother and her affection towards me and devotion to six of us. Once I heard a lecture of a saint in Jain Dharamshala and the wise fellow illustrated the significance of parents in one's life.

He told us — 'Once one of his disciples was not prepared to accept the role of a mother in his life. He tied a stone of 2 kg. weight on his stomach and eventually the disciple failed even to sit for Sadhana and came to him after two hours to remove the stone from his stomach.'

Then the worthy saint told him — 'Your mother nourished you in the womb for nine months and never complained of your weight to anybody. Secondly, the baby feels a lot of pain while coming out of mother's womb and at the same time the labour pains are supposed to be worst as a woman is supposed to push out the baby. Just a day before the womb prepares itself in a natural course for the delivery of the baby and hence opens its mouth a bit larger than usual. Now the disciple accepted the role of a mother in life as people like Karn, Bheem and Arjun are rare. Lords like Rama, Krishna, Buddha and the Tirthankaras have divine powers but their mothers had to bear the labour pains. No mother, no children. She is, like Eve, the creator of people though they get divided in sections, races and nationalities.'

As I took out my handkerchief to wipe my single tear, she asked me — 'What is the matter Pritesh? Why are you so emotional?'

'Just I recollected my mother who might have waited for me in this short break of the college. Nothing else in particular.' I replied.

'You're right. I still cherish the memories of my childhood and early youth when my worthy father narrated me the major events of world history and political developments specially the hostility between India and China and above all between U.S.A. and Russia. He blamed Gorbachev, the Russian leader for the disintegration of Russia into fourteen nations. No state could plan disintegration in the times of former Presidents and Prime Ministers. Actually, we find single political party (Communist Party) in China and Russia and no opposition parties to uproot the government. If anybody tries to raise his/her voice against the system, his/her voice is immediately suppressed. I have read in the newspapers that the Muslims lead a wretched life in China as they fail to form groups there due to the pressure of People's Liberation Army. Young people are generally asked to serve armed forces willy-nilly and can't help the situation.'

Finding me still silent she asked — 'Don't you have interest in world politics? Have you not studied *World History* and *The Discovery of India* written by Pt. J.L. Nehru? As a student you might have studied the salient features of our democracy and the Indian Constitution.'

'Yes, I have studied them but in parts and that too for examination purpose. These days the various Boards of India teach the details of Indian culture, the fundamentals of democracy, growth of capitalism in U.S.A., U.K. and India etc. But then the teachers mostly concentrate on date and number of deaths in two world wars and don't normally discuss the causes and effects of world wars that even Albert Einstein was eager to know.

Secondly, there is a defect in our education system as History teacher does not show the maps of the concerning nations and the Geography teachers don't tell link history with geographical details. As a result, the students get confused between European countries and NATO nations.'

'You're right. But then it is not so in Army Schools where the students are ordered to study major historical events with maps on the boards. Oral questions are raised by the teachers after discussing various events and students are supposed to know the nations existing in Eastern-North, Northern-West, Western-South (or Southern-West) and Southern-East. They are forced to know the terms like latitude and longitude and horizontal and vertical from the geographical points of view.'

'Unfortunately, I have not been taught all this. Teachers have no time to arrange group discussions on socio-political and economic developments. These days the new education policy is being framed for the whole nation. It is unpredictable — What'll be the outcome of that new policy?'

'Quite often the election results are in the mind of policy makers as they are politicians. The intellectuals are in the committee meetings and they have regional issues in mind.'

'Yes. That happens in most of the cases and yet certain good points come out during discussion. As Indian

M

E

D

I

A

is pretty fast, strong and smart, the authorities feel forced to take care of general interest.'

'But madam, a little money is spent on general schools where I studied and my sisters and brothers are studying at the moment.'

'Yes Pritesh, acceptable as you just said. Yet things are coming up. Unfortunately, government's budget is defence oriented rather than education oriented. However, this very system produces I.A.S., I.P.S., P.C.S. officers and intellectuals studying in I.I.T.s and I.I.M.s. Some Law colleges produce wonderful law graduates and post-graduates. Research works are being pursued in abundance and I am told that a few research projects are financed by C.S.I.R. and other organizations. I don't know whether you'll appreciate or condemn the competitions that select best students for top world medical colleges and engineering colleges.'

'But they never think of people like us.'

I lamented and Madam became silent. After two-three minutes she remarked — 'Often I feel that you've communist leanings though communism is a dead force in India except in Kerala.

But don't worry, we both have survived in a capitalist structure, capitalist economy, democracy controlled by capitalists and our politicians generally depend upon the support of these capitalists.'

'Yes. You are right Madam. Why are common people against the economic powers of capitalists? Just voters after every five years. As usual, they find many contestants who don't deserve votes. But the voters can't select their candidates from their town. Then villagers have little voice in the general elections of Parliaments.' I said and she didn't relish what I had remarked.

After a minute she suggested — 'Let's have some rest and lunch in Ludhiana. I have the phone numbers of two blanket manufacturers here. This evening we can talk with them and survey the market. What do you say?'

'As you please'.

□

13

These three days made me feel that anything good and grand could happen with tomorrow. I didn't expect the first day when I played badminton with Madam Shraddha that I would be in her arms after winning two games of badminton. The next tomorrow was again astonishing as we came closer to each other and she offered nice clothes, a wrist watch and a diamond ring to me. This tomorrow was altogether astonishing as I had a lot of money in my name in my bank account. I got a cheque book from the bank and could withdraw money for the fulfilment of my desires. Since I was living with Madam I had no worries about my food and clothing and yesterday she had resolved to start the trading of blankets and shawls to make me feel that I was really employed/self-employed/dependent-employed where the voice of the boss mattered.

I asked her on way to Amritsar — 'Why did you transfer a large amount in my account? What makes you feel insure in life that you nominated me as the second custodian of your locker? Why did you get my name added in F.D.R.s? Why such a haste?'

'No haste dear. You don't know the agony I felt while bidding farewell to my father and father-in-law. Then my husband met car accident and made me a widow. Nothing belongs to us in the real sense as worldly things go on giving us opportunities to do good and bad deeds. In case I am ill now at least you can take care of me and my paralyzed mother. At that time money won't be a problem for you. Of course, you'll be required to get me admitted in the hospital for medical care. Of course, if you analyze this situation, I feel, my love will have his self-dignity and self-respect so as not to feel himself unwanted and a pauper. Of course, you can help your family members as and when you like. They can come and live with both of us and I'll feel delighted in their company as I have no brother, no sisters, no father and my mother is unable to bestow love upon me.'

She became too sad at this moment and changed the programme and parked the car in the parking area of Elphistone Hotel, Ludhiana saying — 'We relax a little in the hotel and then meet two blanket manufacturers after lunch. Come along with me.'

She took a water bottle (boiled water that she drank on visits as these). I followed her and we reached room no. 315 after checking in at the hotel counter. In the meantime, Madam got a call from Yukti who asked about me from her. Madam gave her my cell number and the first call on my mobile was that of Yukti and then I got a call from my younger brother inviting me to visit Panipat. I had become a sort of guest to them.

Since Madam had ordered for two cups of coffee and cookies at the counter, we were served the same in the room. After the waiter had left, madam put off her saree so as to avoid wrinkles on that and was in petticoat and blouse. I went close to her after having coffee and kissed her thighs. She abruptly said — 'Often you think too much. Is it not bad to ignore me? I feel lonely without you.'

'No. But then I think of your whole-self and relish and cherish the memories of last two days. This morning has been quite beyond my expectations. Madam, you are really charming, like Aurora goddess if I may use her name — Ever fresh, ever loving, most benign and ...'

'And what? Don't be panegyric admiring me as beauty is nine days' wonder. Like a wise girl I wish to remain prudent in life. Of course, I find love in your eyes and keep it up Pritesh for love's sake.' She kissed and embraced me passionately.

I took her towards the bed as music was going on in the room. I opened her blouse and her bra and pressed her boobs hard and then the hips. I didn't care for her complain — 'My boobs are aching as you have played with them rather excessively. Please Pritesh.'

Soon we were in the arms of each other and enjoyed the warmth of love. She said — 'I am told by my married friends that honeymoon fever continues at least for six weeks minimum and may continue for six months in most of the cases.'

'Yes. You have rightly heard. Actually, I planned to be in your arms this week but then accepted your proposal to visit Amritsar and Ludhiana. My love fever had just begun as you rightly feel. You know that pure love knows no satiety. The more I resist, the more barrier gets broken'.

She continued to play my organ and kissed my cheeks putting her hand in my hair. I noticed the beauty of her smooth hands and tight thighs and her body created thrill in my body. We made love first on bed and then in the bathtub. As I entered her, she sighed as usual. Of course, she enjoyed the strokes and didn't ask me to stop hitting and I continued to her delight and joy.

After coming out of washroom she slept for half an hour and then ordered for lunch to be served in room. When the waiter knocked at the door, I was in pants, and she hid herself in the washroom and came out after I had bolted the door. She promised to enjoy champagne at night before dinner.

First, we both reached Alpana Woollen Mill and introduced ourselves. We told the manager sales the purpose of our visit. He ordered for cups of coffee and took us to the display hall of blankets and at the same time told the whole-sale price of three varieties of blankets — blankets meant for elite class, for middle class and then the lower sections of society. Commission differed from A, B, C categories and the bulk purchase and minor purchase. Of course, madam calculated in her mind that we could earn 30% on A category blankets, 25% on B quality and 15% to 20% on C category of blankets. He granted us 20% commission on all A, B, C blankets as the order madam gave was for fifty lac rupees. It was decided that the blankets will have the logo of PRITE-SH manufactured in Ambala, not in Ludhiana.

Then the manager created out interest in men's shawls, mostly white, without embroidery and the cost of A, B, C category differed according to the whiteness, butter milk colour, light Coca-Cola colour and then grey colour and of course the weight of the shawl mattered. For each shawl he told us to presume the cost from Rs. 400/- each to Rs. 500/-. Now madam looked towards me for my opinion and ironically I looked at the manager. He understood our dilemma and suggested to buy shawls for thirty lacs (25% returnable if not sold within six months, with 50% less in price). Madam ordered the male shawls for thirty lacs as shawls had become common gifts in most of the institutions and functions.

After that the manager took us to the section of women's shawls and the designs mattered here and not the weight and price. Madam approved roughly fifteen designs and I admired other five designs though I had never bought any so far. Of course, I requested madam in her ear to buy one shawl for my dear mother to be sent through Yukti. She bought one my liking and since madam had ordered shawls for thirty lacs further, the manager got that shawl packed nicely as a gift free of cost.

As we had reached his office, madam offered him another advance cheque of fifty lacs with the promise that the rest of the amount would be sent on delivery. The manager was pretty clever and shrewd and told madam — 'If you are short of money, you can take this cheque back. Ambala is hardly 70 km. away. Whenever you find shortage of any shawl or blanket, intimate me and the required items will be delivered next day. Company trucks manage such things and then the transport service on this Punjab Highway is quite fast. Your requirements will be supplied on top priority. And above all, my sincere good wishes for the success of your business. Madam, you may buy 100 diaries and 100 pens of good quality — One diary and one pen to the buyer of items of five thousand rupees. In diaries you can give our advertisement along with that of yours.'

Madam and I shook hands with him and then reached Veer Woollen Mills. The previous manager had won our heart with his simplicity and made us helpless — No bargains on commissions. Here the manager was alert about the maximum profits of his unit and madam found the opportunity to bargain. Here she liked the synthetic blankets of light weight meant for A.C. rooms. These blankets cost more than A category blankets that we had ordered half an hour ago. Yet madam felt tempted towards ten designs and ordered for five thousand blankets. Then the manager took us to the Lohi Section and madam approved lohi of dark grey colour and ordered for three thousand lohis. Here the Pashmina shawls were wonderful but costly. Yet madam ordered for 500 shawls after seeking my approval regarding designs. We left the factory at 5 P.M. after giving the advance cheque of forty lacs.

Within fifteen minutes we reached the hotel and madam ordered for Malta juice glasses. We had a look at the dining hall facilities which were not very much to her taste. But then she felt delighted seeing the facilities of swimming pool, tennis court, billiards, tennis and badminton. After we had changed in the room, I preferred to play badminton and she opted for tennis first.

She played one singles set of tennis with a tourist who called himself Sandeep Arora. After thirty minutes the set was over and madam entered the badminton court after sipping some more juice. We enjoyed playing two games of badminton and as usual I observed her wholeself while playing the game. Since two spectators had been watching our game, she played superb and defeated me 15-5 and 15-6. This result didn't dishearten me as she had taken part in many competitions and had played several games as hobby. All of a sudden I thought of the difference between the children of ordinary families who have not seen the billiards table and those of officer's families who get government facilities to play and compete with others. But all thought was in vain as who bothered for the interests of lower families!

After playing badminton I wished to return to the room but madam felt tempted for swimming and asked me to enter the pool in my underwear and she entered in her panties and bra. Since there was no other swimmer there, we had free time in blue LED lights and embraced each other in water. We could freely kiss each other and felt refreshed. Finally, we entered the room and took out champagne out of the freeze and ordered for cheese chops and snacks. After the waiter had served the chops and snacks I put my hand round her neck to kiss. But she started discussing — whether we had placed the right orders for woollen items? She had no worry for the money spent so far or for the balance to be paid. She just remarked with questioning eyes — 'I think we have selected the best that was available. Except women's shawls other items are beyond consideration of fashion and no change is going to take place.'

'Soon both of us will learn new selection procedure with experience. I admit, we are new at one time and take the risk.'

'Did you plan for inauguration ceremony Pritesh?' All of a sudden she asked me.

'Not yet. We plan the opening with the end of renovation work and basically Pandit ji will suggest an auspicious date.'

'Will you mind preparing the list of guests for that day? Because date and list are not inter-related.' She suggested.

'Let us finish the first cup and then I write down the names as you suggest. Basically I am a little close to my teacher Dr. Prem Prakash, two boys of my class and then would like to include the names of Yukti, Naini and Kamala Nain.'

'Fine. Write down their names on the sheet of paper.'

Then she dictated roughly fifty names, including the banker, the main tenant of M.B.A. hostel, the city D.M., S.P., G.S.T. Officer, Kotwal, I.T.O., the Sarpanch of her field, etc. By that time she had started feeling tired and asked me to place the order for dinner.

After candle light dinner, I offered prayer to Lord Krishna though it appeared unusual to her as I had not done so on two previous nights. To satisfy her I told her — 'All credit for this success goes to the Lord whether we accept or not.'

'That's right. Om Namah Shivay!'

'Om Namah Shivay!'

We entered the bed and felt the bliss of love once again. Once again she asked me not to press her boobs as there was pain in them. But I had asked the waiter to bring one ointment for that. I told her to move towards me so that I may rub the same there. But she insisted to rub it herself as she expected that I would excite her further.'

'Well, some price has gone to be paid madam! I am ready to serve you at this needed time. It is up to you to accept the courtesy or not.'

'O.K. Do it softly. You make me mad with love.'

'Well, I make love as Cupid might have loved Psyche. Of course, I don't promise to prepare your temple in the outer world. But then your image has settled in these delicate and loving eyes. I can't resist myself. Come closer to me.'

'O.K. As you please.' She embraced me passionately and forgot to discuss the blanket affairs.'

I didn't know about my next tomorrow as yet nor could I guess anything from her gestures and body language.

❒

14

Being tired we went to bed early and madam wanted to enjoy her sleep. But then she saw her husband Vinamra in the dream and the latter called her Gertrude and 'a faithless woman'.

'Hello, my darling! Climax of frailty!' The ghost addressed her.

'Hello dear Vinamra.' Madam replied.

'How am I dear to you?' You have remarried though my ashes have not cooled down. Were you waiting for my death?'

'No. Not at all. I loved you from the depth of heart.' Madam told the ghost.

'Yes. You have forgotten to celebrate my birthday, and didn't offer flowers and sweets to Lord Shiva on Pitra-Amavasya to commemorate the death of my worthy father. Why don't you take care of my sick mother?'

'Sorry, dear. I don't know the rituals and there is no elderly fellow in the family to guide me. I don't mind offering flowers to your picture.' She repented with thirsty throat and felt afraid of the ghost.

'Yes.'

F
A
I
T
H
L
E
S
S

you needed nobody to guide you to surrender yourself to your lover. New honeymoon, inside and outside home. Shameless bitch. He moved his hands towards her throat as if he would strangle her. Madam was terrified badly and cried for help. She got up and made me awake — 'Get up Pritesh. He is here to kill me.'

She was badly sweating though A.C. was on. I tried to console her and brought towel from the washroom to wipe her body. Yet she wept and told me crying — 'How can he blame me? He is dead. How could I survive just with his memories? Why does he want to kill me? What is wrong if I made love to you? Perhaps I have to pay the price of my love to you. I don't bother for traditions and who is he now to force me to follow rituals? Nobody really. No body, no life. His soul ought to get rest as his funeral was properly arranged. I don't know what he needs now?'

And she continued to weep. I tried my best to console her and now took her in my arms saying — 'Perhaps you have seen a bad dream. Dreams are naturally seen by people of all ages in the whole world. Dreams are just illusions and forget the dream that you saw. It is believed that we see dreams when we sleep without digesting our food. Don't weep. Nobody can harm you. You are brave, madam and I am with you. Nobody can strangle you. See, nobody is here.' Night lamp had already been switched on.

'Yes. His soul appeared to curse me and blame me. Maybe his soul failed to get peace after death. It was actually an untimely and premature death. But then I am not to be blamed for his death or the death of his Papa.' She still wept and I wiped her tears.

I told her — 'Try to forget the contents of death. Sorry, I was fast asleep.'

'No. It's alright. You may sleep. I disturbed you for nothing.' She felt sorry.

But I took her close to my heart and kissed her shoulders and cheeks saying — 'You can trust your Pritesh. You have committed no unethical crime. Nothing to be ashamed of!'

She felt a little relieved of her tension when I continued to kiss her cheeks. She tried to forget the dark memories that had suddenly captured her mind.

'Don't feel tense on any account. Feel free to speak if something is hurting you still. All will be over and your grief will wither away in my company.' I tried my best to pacify her injured heart.

'Try to fight against the ghost. Maybe it is your presumption that the ghost of your husband appeared before you to strangle you. Just a shadow of a shadow may be there to make you feel so nervous. After all, you are the daughter of army officer. How can you cry like a child? No way. Feel yourself bold enough to fight against all oddities. Quite often our sentiment appears before us in the dream and makes us weep and cry. If you recollect Lady Macbeth and Macbeth saw terrible dreams.'

'But I am no lady Macbeth. I didn't plan his accident. He died of his own carelessness, drunk as he was. He has no right to blame me for his death. No. No way.'

'Sorry to refer to Lady Macbeth and Macbeth. Try to sleep.'

As she was close to my chest, I rubbed her hips and thighs and finally kissed her boobs. She was coming out of her trauma and the worst was over. She didn't mind when I rubbed her boobs and perhaps the cream had given relief to her. Since she felt a little excited now, she embraced me passionately and I too wanted to divert her attention.

She was struggling to come out of her fear and then kissed me asking — 'Will you continue loving me dear?'

'Sure. Nothing to doubt. How can you survive as a lonely lady? You need the right kind of emotional support and I am there with you all times. No reason to doubt my faithfulness. After all, we have taken certain decisions.'

'Yes. I ought not to doubt you. Come closer.'

'Yes. I am already close to you.'

I kissed her and rubbed her here and there and her front area.

Since I felt excited after rubbing her I found she too was passionate and I entered her and pressed her boobs. She enjoyed the amorous affair and had no fear and tear on her face. I gave her strokes and that added to her pleasure and finally we came together. After coming out of washroom she possessed me as she didn't want any kind of fear. We tried to sleep forgetting the dream.

She was almost normal in the morning and we enjoyed joint bath in the washroom. Last night I felt enthusiastic about city Amritsar due to the Golden Temple as I had heard much of its spiritual glory and divine splendour. This tomorrow was going to fulfil my long-cherished ambition. I wondered how could the noble Sikhs manage this much of gold? I was going to get the reply of my questions. Madam had been there several times and told me lot about the pilgrims and film stars that came there to offer regards and tribute to the Nine Saints of the Panth.

After bath madam took out the brass statue of Lord Krishna and lighted perfume sticks. Then both of us offered prayers to Lord Krishna and she prayed in her heart to seek His blessings in times of fear. She felt sorry as if she had committed any crime in her life.

But to her surprise she heard a divine sound — 'Maa'.

She failed to realize and understand — who was there apart from me? Who had called her 'Maa'?

She was half-way between engagement and marriage as we both had not taken seven rounds of fire. No shlokas had been recited and no flower garlands had been exchanged so far. No blessings of my parents had been sought and yet she was being called — 'Maa'.

She asked — 'Did you listen any sound? Who is the third person here to make such false sound? Yes, somebody is here invisible perhaps!'

I pacified her putting my hand on her shoulder and told her — 'Madam, try to come out of the fear of dream. No sense in feeling hallucinations. Fear is a bad companion whatever shape it takes. You're after all rational, prudent and logical. Room is closed and door bolted. Then who can be here? Perhaps you are still in trauma of the dream.'

She took out her pistol and put it on the back of her jeans. I was totally taken aback seeing the pistol. After taking breakfast she told me 'We can start our trading with these purchases and may visit Amritsar some time else. What is the hurry? It will be cold after two-three weeks.'

She proposed and asked the receptionist to manage for a driver to drop us in Ambala.

Before the driver was arranged, she got bad news on her phone from the warden of M.B.A. hostel that her young sister-in-law (Mirdul, 18) had been raped and killed though she was being looked after by a guard Santa and perhaps she had died three days ago. Due to bad smelling the warden made the phone call and asked her to hurry up. She told him to wait for two hours as she was out of station.

Then she contacted Sarpanch of her village to be in contact with the police of Ambala so that the event does not take a political twist. Let the Kotwal be satisfied that Mirdul was mentally retarded and the guard looked after her well. She had been under lock and key as she often became very violent and hence unbearable. Madam felt sad at first and lamented — 'O my God! Who could rape and kill such a girl? Can people behave so roughly with half-mad girls? Are even mad girls not safe in the town?'

She told me the details of Mirdul on way back. This was my fourth tomorrow with sad news of murder and rape. All the way she didn't leave my right hand as unexpected tragedy had happened. She knew that she might be in trouble if police officer didn't help her. The students living in the hostel must have seen her disfigured body and the situation might take a serious turn. After all, rape and murder are no ordinary issues and she found herself helpless and insecure.

'My God! Please help me in this critical situation. Elderly people die leaving the responsibilities upon me — poor me. I am already having a new terrible experience. This has added fuel to fire. O Mirdul! What a bad time have you chosen for me? I never had any free time in the last four months, one tragedy after another. What a result of my previous birth's deeds! How long to suffer?'

I consoled her in the car and asked her to concentrate upon police action and if she deemed proper, to contact a criminal lawyer for the event. He will manage the police and help us in giving the statements. Then she asked the Sarpanch to bring an advocate too.

Sarpanch and the advocate Sharma ji narrated the incident to the Kotwal and did the needful. As a result, two constables arrived on the spot and the dead body was handed over to us after filing the Panchnama without much arguments. Madam had to confirm her long mental illness and the warden confirmed her insanity. Thanks God, there was no enquiry — How it all happened? Who had raped her? No postmortem of the body and Mirdul's dead body was put on the funeral pyre and madam asked me to light the fire. I knew her mental condition and hence silently obeyed her.

Whatever money was lying in Mirdul's Bank A/c was all donated to the local orphans by madam.

'Another death in the family!'

She lamented at night.

15

This day I had expected to see the Golden Temple and the Jallianwala Bagh but unexpected news of Mirdul made me a little sad. As a young man, it was my first chance to shoulder a pyre and then light the funeral pyre. Good for nothing. So far my worthy father had never allowed me to join any funeral procession but here I was helpless. Of course, I was nobody to poke my nose in this affair and felt sad in the bungalow. Madam had severe head-ache though there was no police fear and Sarpanch came to her to console her — 'Everything is O.K. Don't worry madam. We can have her chotha in the field and I'll manage the whole affair.'

Madam left me, took out some money from the drawer and paid to Sarpanch saying — 'See that it is all set properly.'

'Yes. I'll make a phone call if needed.'

'Fine. Thanks.' And Sarpanch left giving her mental relief.

Yet she felt herself sad and asked the maidservant to prepare salad and took out bottles of Vodka and Gin, mixed them up in two glasses, added ice cubes and hinted me to give company. In this moment of her anguish I could not turn down her request and took the glass silently.

In a sweet soft voice she said — 'Cheers Pritesh. It is one hallucination after another. Who was that devil that raped Mirdul?

She had not cheated anybody to suffer like this. Saddest thing is that her dead body was seen by the warden after two-three days of murder. Will humanity survive in this Kalayug or not? Perhaps the time has arrived for Lord Krishna to take care of his devotees.'

I told her mildly — 'Who are we to guide the Lord? He'll do everything of his own. Maybe Mirdul was fated to die unnatural death like this. Who can predict? She had already suffered a lot since childhood. Cases of mental illness, insanity, half-madness, etc. have been growing regularly. Who knows if she had dementia on account of loneliness? Guard is to be doubted because Mirdul had grown young. The students of M.B.A. were discussing about her beauty which instigated the guard or some student to have sex with her. For fear of revelation she might have been killed by the rapist. But madam, this is all guess work.'

'Yes. I'm not in a position to contest any legal case because nothing can be achieved without much serious efforts. No wisdom contesting this case. She died as Lord desired.' She took another sip and then we dined together with lips shut.

It was a different kind of night and we were half-sad though her death was a relief to her retarded mind. She was sad when she entered the bed in her nighty and came closer to me on account of her sense of insecurity. She said — 'Thanks Pritesh for all cooperation in today's performance. Had I been alone, I would have fainted with helplessness and grief. You saved me in the real sense and I'll of course, remember this act of kindness. Of course, it was not lip sympathy and no cold shoulders to the funeral pyre.'

I kissed her hand and said — 'It is just O.K. Nobody knows what'll happen the next minute. My first meetings with you were all fated by good luck. Yukti took me here and we felt interested in each other though I was no good player of badminton. Try to forget the funeral ethics as it'll add to your panic.'

'Yes. You're right.' She embraced me tightly to feel sure that I was in bed with her. Love proved to be the best relief from panic that she had faced in the last eighteen hours.

Next morning I got a call from my brother Ajoy who invited me to celebrate Diwali in the new Spring Apartments where my whole family had shifted. I was told about his jewellery shop by Yukti and I felt surprised. Today it was further surprising to know that my family members bought two apartments. He gave me house number and told me — 'All remember you Bhai. Do join us celebrate Diwali in this new house. Take care of your studies and Papa and Mummy send their good wishes for your future. I am sorry I could not study. But then God's wishes have got to be obeyed. Namastey Bhai.'

It was a pleasant surprise that parents could buy new apartments. I expected brother might have bought new furniture. After all, he was growing young. He too was of marriageable age. Maybe Papa arranges his marriage first as mine is uncertain. But the word

U
N
C
E
R
T
A
I
N

hit me hard as I was half-married, enjoying all possible comforts and physical pleasures of live-in-relationship.

Shraddha had seriously told me that she had taken three steps towards me i.e.

Surrendered her body to me.

Got me nominated for her locker.

Transferred a lot of money in my name and added my names in F.D.R.s.

Of course, it was my turn to move towards her but then I thought uselessly —

(a) I too had surrendered my whole-self to her.

(b) Now I loved her for the sake of love.

(c) I loved her without the permission of my parents and was supposed to face my parents now. Maybe she didn't think of this issue at all. She could regard me selfish as I planned business when the doors of Professorship were almost closed.

I had rightly heard that God Himself opens the last door when ninety nine doors are closed. Of course, the door was almost open and I was to prove my worth with hard work. In business, I am told, one has to devote time to trade affairs forgetting all personal pleasures. But then madam was with me as 24×7 company and I could depend upon her prudence and wisdom.

I was not foolish to regard myself as madam's partner on 50% basis because all the investments had been made by her. Of course, she was generous enough to give my name on the logo of our trade.

In the last two days the contractor had tiled the two floors of ground floor and walls were to be tiled 4' high. This morning tiling began on first floor where we were supposed to shift after a week or so. Due to her enthusiasm she asked the plumber concerned to use the best Parry wares and Jaquar fittings. Designs of wash rooms were finalized by her and there was attached washroom with each room.

Madam got the phone number of one of members of club to appoint his nephew as computer operator and she interviewed him after half an hour. I saw that fifteen almirahs had reached the bungalow yesterday and the guard put them in the third room. The two rooms that had been tiled, were cleaned properly as the blankets, shawls etc. were supposed to be kept in each here next day. The computer operator was explained his role in the trade and he needed another operator and an attendant. Madam took care of that and did the needful.

The electrician had installed eight LED tubes, two air-conditioners and three fans in each room. The technician to do aluminium panel work had reached with his team of two skilled labourers and madam directed him to do the needful. This is how business took a start, a start-up.

Since madam's father, father-in-law and husband had been in the army, she knew many influential officers. Some of her class friends got appointed in Defence and were still in her touch. To my surprise one Brigadier who had earlier been friend of her father promised to buy five thousand blankets as first purchase. This is how, there was nothing to worry about. After getting the order on e-mail, there was no limit to our joy and madam proposed for celebration.

That evening was superb and we both missed the company of Yukti, Naini and Kamala Nain. She opened the bottle champagne after playing badminton. Then we had two cups of champagne. And as she was in a mood to play billiards, both of us played billiards for half-an-hour. But before the game began, she warned me — 'Hit the ball, not the table's cloth or else cloth gets torn. Take care of Pritesh as it is your first chance.'

'Yes. It is my first chance to play with wood balls. But I have learnt a lot playing with fleshy balls in the last three days.'

'Oh, don't be silly.' She remarked with a smile.

She guided my hands to hit the balls well and eventually I could play with some confidence. She won as she had won my whole-self. I had no regrets for losing the game and thanked her to make me play billiards.

After playing billiards I recollected the experience of new born skylark who had flown beyond his capacity and physical strength. Sitting on the branch of a tree far off his nest he recollected his fellow family members and thought that they would miss him that evening. He felt hungry too. Yet he tried to fly again and once again but fell down.

Two swallows were seeing this effort of small skylark and reached the branch where the baby skylark was sitting. They told him sarcastically 'Foolish bird, why did you fly far off if you didn't know the art of flying a long distance. This is the tragedy of many new birds like you who imitate birds like us that cross even ocean. I didn't, as you did, ever try to surpass my physical limits.'

After that one swallow flew naturally and came back to that baby-skylark saying — 'Did you notice how to fly? Learn the skill of flying first and then fly in future.'

Then the swallows flew again and returned the same branch to their surprise, the skylark had learnt the lesson of flying with the two flights of swallows and could manage to fly again.

The sarcastic remarks of two swallows had proved helpful for the baby-skylark and gave her self-confidence.

I thought of myself as a baby bird in business who had advanced many steps though my investments were zero. The only qualities of my personality were obedience, tolerance, righteousness and prudence as I wanted to stand on my legs. I had no other friend or family relation who could help me establish even a business of one thousand rupees. I found that my B.A. degree was almost a sheet of paper and could not make me earn my bread even for a month. How long could I depend upon my poor parents for eleven years, doing research and then preparing for N.E.T.? Just then I stood before the statues of Lord Shiva and Lord Krishna for help. What can't a man do with God's blessings? I thought and moved towards the dining table for dinner.

◻

16

Next day was pretty busy as tiling was going on first floor and the computer operator Mr. Arpit Singhal (33) had joined the job. A few registers were bought from the market with a ledger. Steel hoarding with PRITE-SH Shawls and Blankets had been ordered. Ten more steel almirahs reached the bungalow and the third room was considered suitable for keeping the stocks. Aluminium Glass doors were being prepared. With the arrival of almirahs the gardener asked madam to appoint his son Ronny (19) as an attendant though he was just Intermediate. For this job a highly qualified man was not required. Due to blankets and costly shawls madam appointed another guard (50) retired from the army and guns were given to both of them. Madam got her father-in-law's pistol released from the Police Station Ambala and asked me to practice shooting.

Madam was well aware of growing crime rate in the area and as captain's daughter was extra conscious of her security. She suggested me to learn driving as I may drive when she is ill or out of station for business. When the trainer informed her of my lack of interest in driving, she appointed young driver Arjun (22) for my help. She wanted that my life should be equally fast and energetic. Mobility had become a slogan of 21st century.

This afternoon she suggested me to listen to videos from you-tube as many lectures on various books and authors had been uploaded upon the website. That way I would be in touch with books that I was interested in. Some videos were regarded really useful by her and she told a few titles that she admired most.

In the evening Yukti reached the bungalow along with Naini and Kamala Nain. She was delighted to see me but failed to understand — How did I feed myself in this short break? She told me that she had met my parents in the new house and my brother had furnished the same.

Madam asked me to play with Yukti, Naini and Kamala Nain as she had to take care of the renovation work. Inventory of blankets was being prepared and the computer operator, his assistant, and the attendant were busy with that. Yet madam wanted to have a look — how the blankets were being put by the attendant?

Yukti had a tough fight against me this evening as I had practised a lot in this break and madam had given me tips to improve my game. After playing second game with Naini I came out of the court and asked them to continue playing. Yukti, Naini and Kamala Nain played two games each and then Yukti, as expected, asked me — 'Hello hero. Which author did you prepare in these days?'

'Nothing in particular.' I simply replied.

'Your answer is sheer disgusting. You stayed back for preparation of notes. Now to my surprise and shock, you tell me, nothing in particular. Did you continue to play with balls and shuttlecocks? I know your nature and you'll never waste your time. I know for sure.' Yukti was justified but I promised to discuss the issue with her later on. But she insisted — 'What's wrong with you?'

'Nothing in particular.'

I tried to evade the issue and joined madam for coffee. Finally, all the three girls left almost dissatisfied with my dry answer. But then I could not share the secret of my new relationship with madam as girls hardly keep any secret.

Since Dhania brought her young daughter Chanchal (18) to be a helping hand in the kitchen, we both got coffee prepared by this new arrival. This young girl was bewitching and had a slim body and fair complexion with developed boobs. She had filled examination form for B.A. Part I with English literature, History and Economics. She wished to follow the theory earn while you learn, so popular among the young girls of Haryana. She was supposed to stay in the bungalow at night so that she might prepare tea/coffee at odd hours. But she had been entrusted the hard work of dusting and wiping the floors. She was ready to work on monthly salary of ten thousand rupees, plus food and clothing.

Next tomorrow brought the wonderful news of a semi-large wooden box that had been lying locked in the store of Mirdul's room. Due to carving on its outer sides it was superb after dust was removed by Dhania. The warden had been asked by madam to get that room repaired, whitewashed and painted. The painter had told the warden about this heavy box that the guard Santa might not have seen. It had a big lock upon it and had not been opened for years. Since Mirdul had survived in that lonely room, madam too had never visited that.

With the help of a blacksmith the lock was broken without spoiling the shape of the box and the blacksmith was paid his fee and sent back home. Then madam shut the door after thanking the warden and opened the box — It was a moment of wonder and she took it to be Pandora's Box, with feelings of fear and wonder. As she opened the lid, we both were surprised to find a lot of gold ornaments that madam's father-in-law might have kept safe for the future of Mirdul. The late army officer loved the dignity of his house and didn't wish her to be a burden upon anybody financially. Since his pension account was operated by madam, he was pretty sure that she would take care of a mentally sick girl and that madam had always done.

I recollected the incident when my mother gave her two gold bangles to my Papa to sell for my education. But I found it unwise to ask madam for two bangles out of this collection of gold ornaments. Since I had no right upon them, I remained silent and waited for the reaction of madam. At first sight she exclaimed — great God, how prudent my father-in-law was! He didn't offer me this much gold in my marriage. Anyway, his land and house got transferred in my name. It is enough as it is. Why to cry over spilt milk — one bird in the hand is better than two in the bush.

Mr. S.K. Arora, a retired Lieutenant from Defence had often requested her for the improvement and renovation of local orphanage and now madam made phone call to him saying — 'Arora, the orphanage can be renovated now. Meet me at your gate as I am coming with the contractor. As guardian of orphans please talk to the social welfare officer for his permission. God willing, the orphans would have good living conditions. Rest when we visit the sight.'

Madam put all those ornaments in my wooden almirah and asked me to lock it. Then she talked with the contractor who had been looking after tiling in this bungalow and asked me to take care of blanket affair and left for orphanage. Since gold was being sold now @ of fifty thousand rupees per ten gram, she hoped to get roughly fifty lac rupees from the sale of these ornaments.

The contractor saw the old shattered building of orphanage and needed fifteen lacs for fifteen rooms, plus two lacs for washrooms. But madam consulted Lieutenant Arora — 'Will you mind if we leave walls unplastered. All construction will be done with good cement and stone dust. Floors will be prepared with cement. We can get the building plastered later on. The contractor will demolish four rooms first, construct them specially using red stones and steel garters for the roof, with aluminium doors. That way we can get fourteen rooms constructed and I'll manage all the construction cost. Arora ji was fully mesmerized with this philanthropic gesture of madam. The project was finalized within minutes and next day the work began. Madam planned to visit the site after every three days and gave a cheque of two lac rupees to Arora ji.

I didn't expect such philanthropy from her. Any greedy woman would have kept the ornaments for herself as they were almost relics to my mind. But madam was built of a different stuff, merciful as she was. She had no mind to win any election. She never aspired for any post in the Ambala Club or any other social organization. She didn't buy any black/white stone to put on the wall of orphanage and asked Arora ji to keep her name a secret. Why to invite trouble from Income Tax and the police department — they might ask — 'How did you get this much amount?'

Madam hoped to get the rooms constructed within a month. Pullovers, shirts and pants were offered to the orphans. Two guys were appointed on monthly salary of fifteen thousand each to teach these orphans. I recollected William Shakespeare's words — 'Mercy blesses both — giver and the receiver.'

◻

17

While waiting for dinner to be served by Chanchal, I told madam — 'Your beauty captures my attention all the time.'

'And your decent personality makes me mad Pritesh.' She was quite witty and could reply my comments, accepting their validity.

She added — 'Go on watching my beauty forever and forever and you'll get my love as a response for that. I love you Pritesh though I make no demands from you.'

After sipping tomato juice she left the chair and took my hand to get up and we entered the bedroom. She embraced me tightly and looking into my eyes asked passionately — 'Will you marry me today or tomorrow? I'll die without you. Please don't postpone the matter as we have known each other, understood each other and of course you have brought bloom in my desert.'

She waited for my answer and it was a question of life and death for her. She didn't want to express my passion for her — her real-self now.

'Yes, right now or tomorrow.'

Then she bolted the door and both of us kissed each other. Then we came out of room to light the lamp and the fragrance sticks before Lord Shiva and Lord Krishna. Everything happened unplanned as she analyzed my remark about her beauty and I thought of her. I didn't bother for the permission of parents and became highly conscious of my poverty. My choice for college Professorship appeared to be a cry in the wilderness, all futile and not worth paying attention for. Yukti and Dipali could afford it but not poor me.

I was poor not because my parents owed money to anybody or were under any financial burden. But then Papa used to tell me — 'Look Pritesh, remember you are supposed to earn for yourself and secondly help me in the marriage of your sisters. I'll be retiring after six years.'

This request of Papa was sincere and all parents have their expectations from their children. I hoped to be a dedicated son to him but was not prepared to die with the arrows of Time, Fate and financial crisis as the dedicated son Shravana Kumara had died with the arrow of king Dasharatha.

Lovingly madam told me — 'We enjoy honeymoon now and have seven rounds of fire tomorrow just to obey the rituals otherwise we have lived these four days as a couple.'

She kissed me hard and unbuttoned my shirt and unzipped my jeans. And she said — 'Now you appear a smart young guy suitable for any smart girl.'

'Smart in your eyes madam and suitable for you only. I am no philanderer to seek love in the eyes of every young girl. That way I will be false to you as well as to myself. I have been fortunately brought up in a different atmosphere and in our family the chastity of males is as important as the virginity of girls. Rest assured madam.'

'Superb darling. It was expected of you. I know I have committed no mistake to select you for myself. It is just by chance that you got defeated in badminton but won me, my heart and soul for yourself.'

I kissed her and removed her shirt and skirt that she had been wearing since morning. This night love-making started a bit earlier. As I entered her, she gave a warning — 'Enjoy making love tonight as I have my monthly period day after tomorrow.'

'Yes. No worry. Period does not take my princess far away from me. We can still enjoy kissing, embracing and sleeping together.' I assured her without feeling tense about her monthly period as it was a monthly routine with every young girl.

Finally, I entered her and she didn't moan and sigh as she used to. She overpowered me and came upon me to give me strokes. What a change! She felt delighted as we were getting married tomorrow. She knew for sure that I had not taken permission from parents for my marriage with her. But she thought it to be my responsibility as I was in her company and made love in her arms. Love won all obstacles, as we felt.

While playing with her boobs I recollected William Shakespeare's *Antony And Cleopatra* and thought — Julius Caesar and Antony must have rubbed Cleopatra's boobs like I did now. When Antony was requested by his subordinate officer to return to Rome for the safety of his native land, he aptly said :

"Let Rome in Tiber melt and the wide arch

Of the ranged empire fall. Here is my space.

Kingdoms are clay."

And the brave Roman forgot his honour for his beloved Cleopatra and didn't bother for Fulvia as well as Octavia.

I could love my ever fresh Aurora as I was not old like her lover Tithonus. Like Yayati, I had passion for love and sex and knew how to make love with princess of my heart. My youth was in full bloom and we both needed each other to feel satisfied.

As I entered her, she asked me — 'You are not getting married under any pressure, I suppose. If you feel not interested in me, you can still say no.' She pleaded.

First, I kissed her cheeks and then gave stroke. After two minutes she had melted out of confusion and doubt and repeated her question. I told her — 'No question to doubt each other anymore. The stage for such question has already been crossed by us. Enjoy these moments as we are close to each other's heart. Since I had no doubts, I never asked such questions from you. Fine darling.'

After early bath we dressed ourselves in best attire and I put on the white terricot suit with black tie. She wore silken saree and Pandit ji reached the bungalow at 9 A.M. Mr. Singhal and his assistant, the guards, the gardener and his maid Dhania and her daughter Chanchal and of course the Sarpanch had been requested to bless us. Without any formalities of Haldi ceremony and Mehndi-rituals, Pandit ji recited the shlokas and we took seven rounds of fire with full dedication and sincerity.

Lunch had been ordered at Loretto restaurant for fifteen people and all the spectators enjoyed the occasion and both of us felt assured of ourselves as husband and wife as I had put vermilion in the middle of her hair. The Sarpanch and Mr. Singhal were formal and brought gifts for us. The labourers were given sweets so as to mark the occasion. Fruits were sent to orphans through Mr. Singhal. To my surprise there was a new Honda City car parked in front of the bungalow and she offered me the keys after others had left. I kissed her hand when I got the keys and thanked her for another act of generosity. But I failed to resist myself and told her — 'Your other gifts were enough. You know that I don't know driving. Anyway thanks a lot.'

'Yes. I know you don't know driving a car. But the driver has been appointed this morning only. You may learn driving with his help. Even if you feel scared of driving the driver will be available 24×7 for us.'

Madam told me — 'She planned to build six servant rooms, with kitchen and washroom in the south of bungalow. That way servants will be available the whole day and night.'

'Not to worry about driving.' She had a bird's eye view of tiling and inventory affair and then we reached our bedroom.

She just switched on A.C, and told me kissing — 'Today you look superb like the last Viceroy of India Lord Mountbatten. Remain smart darling as you are my bonafide boss now.'

And she kissed on my cheeks.

This tomorrow had started passing though I had become a responsible husband. I half-realized my new duties towards her, trading and other homely affairs. The ground floor appeared to be topsy-turvy as a few items had been put in the corners of bed rooms and even the drawing room. Yet I hoped to find myself settled soon in new furnished bedroom on first floor.

Seeing the advertisements of a few furniture companies, madam ordered for a new bed, new wall sofa, new dining table etc. As the first floor two rooms got ready the new furniture was put there and the room appeared glamorous. A.C. had already been installed along with new electric fittings.

Before taking lunch madam made phone to some Brigadier Tiwari to seek his blessings for new life and new trade. Since Mr. Tiwari had been a close friend of her father, he had attended her marriage ceremony and also sent condolence letter on the death of Vinamra. First, he told her that he was damn pleased to talk to her. Then he congratulated her on getting married. But then he asked her to supply five thousand heavy wool blankets and check the quality with Veer Woollen Mills. He told her to send the quotations on-line with Re. 1/- less than the previous rates.

It was a pleasant news for us both as we got the order for bulk supply. After lunch madam sent the driver to Ludhiana with item number and purchased a dozen blankets so that the owners don't doubt us. We were happy in bed and madam told me — 'I just made a courtesy call to uncle Tiwari. Unexpectedly he proved to be a boon in disguise. Now we buy these five thousand blankets in other name and then put our logo upon them and supply to Jammu Regiment. Is that not great?'

'Yes darling. It is very good news to be celebrated.'

And then we celebrated our real honeymoon without fear of social criticism. Next tomorrow madam herself referred to my parents — 'Had your parents been here, we would have been blessed by them too.'

'Nothing to worry. We go to Panipat one day before Diwali and see what happens there. Of course, I could not be dishonest to my love on account of my parents.' I told her and kissed her hand to assure her of my sincerity.

◻

18

I retired to drawing room after playing a single game with Yukti. This evening madam was busy in the salesroom and checked various tags as attached by the company. Her driver had brought the new blankets from Veer Woollen Mills and she had ordered for five thousand blankets without any logo of the mill. She was busy with business affair as she was

E
N
T
H
U
S
I
A
S
T
I
C

about each aspect of the trade. Sitting alone I just recollected the faces of my parents and wished to see them with madam. I was unable to feel that the meeting would be nice or unwanted in Panipat home. My brothers and sisters may approve or disapprove my marriage. I thought of the question — How would madam face the hard reality there? Will she keep silent in hostile situation or react boldly or leave them alone and drive back to Ambala in an instant. I asked myself — Why did I not try to seek their permission before getting married? Was it too late to bow down before them for accepting her? What gifts should be bought along with sweets and fruits? I felt confused and found no wisdom consulting madam on this issue. Then the idea hit me — I can first visit them alone and invite them for the inauguration ceremony of Sales Room to be held after three days.

It was going to be grand day as Brigadier Pandey of Ambala Cantt. had given his consent to inaugurate the Sales Room/Show Room. But he had told madam to be punctual as he would stay only for fifteen minutes, have a cup of black coffee and then leave without any formality. I too was enthusiastic about the proposed arrival of D.M.'s wife that evening.

It was just the beginning of romance in my married life and there was no lack of warmth from either side. Marriage was not the end of our love-story and I regarded it the beginning of a new life. Maybe madam was trying to repair her youth but she tried to avoid the incidents of her first marriage. Where did she enjoy her honeymoon? What were her adventures worth narrating me?

When I was lost in these thoughts Yukti came to the drawing room and sat by my side. With a sad face she asked me — 'Do you know about the new developments in your family at Panipat?'

'No. I have no idea except that my brother has managed a jewellery shop. I don't know from where he got the money? Then my parents have shifted to apartments. That is all. Is there anything wrong there?'

'Yes. Things are wrong with your sister Toshi. She was kidnapped on 23rd September 2019 by a group of three rascals. Not only this they kidnapped her two friends Kammo (17) and Shanu (17) along with her. They put three of them in a deserted godown of a company on Jind road.'

'Then?' I asked with anxiety. Kidnappers, so far as I know, were Talu, Birju and Bhandari. Bhandari was asked to take care of these three innocent girls and their hands were tied on their back. Bhandari had a stolen pistol and his accomplices Talu and Shanu went in search of other girls as their target was to kidnap at least ten girls that day. Bhandari felt hungry and drank almost half bottle of whisky and then ate food.

These three girls had received Judo training and were the best cadets of N.C.C. Toshi and Kammo are first-rate shooters of N.C.C. Due to their struggle for self-defence, Toshi could take out her hands from the knot of cord and without wasting any second hit Bhandari and he fell on his back. She took his pistol and killed him. Then she freed her friends Kammo and Shanu.

'Then anything else?'

'Yes. It was the beginning of the whole affair. Talu and Birju wanted to take revenge from Toshi and were seen near your home next day at 5 P.M. or so. Since Toshi recognized these rascals she, perhaps, fired two shots and killed both of them. This created panic in the street and the sub-inspector of police reached the spot with a jeep full of constables. Since the rascals fell with bullet shots, it was not fully clear — who had fired at them? What was the purpose of this murder story? A thorough search of your area was taken but pistol could not be recovered. Nobody expected such revenge from girls specially as the episode of kidnapping was not revealed to parents by these girls.'

'And then?'

'Well, L.I.U. Inspector knew a little about kidnapping of girls. But he too didn't know which particular girls had been kidnapped and why? Actually, the crime rate had been growing in the town since last year. Prostitution, abduction, kidnapping, murder, violence and chauth have become common features. People feel themselves unsafe.'

'Is Toshi safe now? What about her friends? Are they safe now?' I asked and felt nervous and encouraged with the bravery of my sister who was nearly 16 years of age.

Toshi added — 'After two days two pimps who had forced innocent poor girls in flesh-trade were unexpectedly killed from a distance of fifteen yards. One of them was Thakur something and the media has raised questions about the inaction of police. Who could kill the pimps so cleverly? L.I.U. tried to find out but no results.'

'Well, vagabonds got justice of their evil deeds.' I told her.

But Yukti informed me — 'I am told that Shiva and Reeva used to take chauth from every truck going out of Panipat and coming in the town. Truck drivers were fed up with this affair. Three days after the murder of pimps, Shiva and Reeva were killed with bullets and the police officers have yet failed to arrest the culprit. The main question before them is that of pistol that has been used thrice by the shooters.'

'But how does Toshi come into picture?'

'Because L.I.U. and the City Kotwal take it for granted that Toshi has fired shots all three times. Almost everyday the L.I.U. Inspector or senior constable or sub-inspector visits your home to get the pistol. But Toshi has become pretty bold these days as she might have taken inspiration from Jhansi Ki Rani, Madam Kiran Bedi or even Indira Gandhi. Her classmates confirm that she had often admired even Phoolan Devi in the conversation with girls. Since the police officers have not recovered the pistol, they can't proceed further for enquiry. S.S.P. Karnal has been putting due pressure upon S.P. City (Panipat) to enquire the details of these three episodes. But the best part is that many anti-social elements and rogues have left the town lest they should be shot down dead.'

I sighed to hear all these tragic episodes but doubted that my sister, so homely and innocent could dare to kill pimps and chauth collectors. I thought that three episodes were different and there was no common point in them. If my sister had really killed the evil-doors she needed my moral support at every cost. After all, she was my sister-blood is thicker than water. I felt fully disturbed but then failed to disclose all this to madam lest she should form a bad idea about my sister specially.

On every Raksha Bandhan festival I promised my sisters to help and protect them. Of course, Mummy could afford Rs. 5/- for each sister for three brothers, Toshi complained and wanted Rs. 5/- for each of us. But mother pacified saying that brothers will pay more when they earn. That way sisters waited for the years when their brothers earned. Mother prepared kheer as it was a ritual.

I thought of the times when I used to teach English to my younger brothers and sisters. Except Ajoy, others paid attention to what I taught. Toshi was very intelligent as she learnt many idioms, antonyms and homophones. She learnt tenses with full attention and could help the younger sister. As Kammo's father was teacher of Economics, she enjoyed her company. As Kammo had developed the habit of speaking in English, Toshi felt all the more intimate with her.

Both the friends had won many awards in debates and often their pictures got printed in local newspapers *Amar Ujala* and *Dainik Jagran* and *The Tribune*. Their principal knew them well as they had won Haryana trophy in N.C.C. and debates. Other girls took inspiration from these two friends and formed Gandhi Debating Society. My sister Toshi could recite English poems written by Sarojini Naidu and Swami Vivekananda and that won the heart of lovers of English verses.

In High School Toshi wished to be a Tehsildar as she thought that Tehsildar is the best and most powerful officer since Papa worked under his control. But then her vision widened in intermediate and she aspired to be P.C.S. officer while studying for XII exams. My books of Social Science (a compulsory subject up to High School in Haryana) proved highly useful for all brothers and sisters. We used to ask questions from each other —

(a) Which author wrote the particular book?

(b) Which poet wrote the particular poem and when?

(c) Which dramatist/novelist wrote the particular drama/ novel and when?

(d) Toshi often asked me to tell her the details of Renaissance Movement, Restoration of Charles II, French Revolution, Industrial Revolution, Bolshevik Revolution and Information Revolution. Of course, she quoted these major events in her speeches.

(e) There used to be purposeful competition about the titles of books beginning with each English Letter and Hindi Letter. Days of

       F

       R

       E

       E

C
H
I
L
D
H
O
O
D

were fully delightful and there was no feeling of mine and thine in the family. Of course, there was no furniture in the house but we never aspired for that. There were two fans (one ceiling fan and one table-fan) in my home.

I recollected all this after Yukti had left and madam became free. I felt highly worried about the present and future of my sister and other family members. This evening only I didn't hope for the early arrival of night to make romance with beloved madam.

'Man proposes and God disposes.'

◪

19

I failed to decide what to do now. How to help Toshi and share the grief of my parents whom I had ignored in my marriage! Parents normally had big enthusiasm about the marriage of their eldest son. But that had been denied to them by me. But then they had no idea about the situation as I had crushed my ambition to be a college Professor. In business everything was uncertain and secondly both of us had no experience of trading. However, Madam had regular income from pension of her husband and she was supposed to lose it due to her marriage with me. With on-line message she had informed the treasury about her marriage. But then the rent of the M.B.A. hostel was there every month.

I failed to decide what to reveal and hide from her. But then murder and theft are at last out. When I reached the dining table and maid served me vegetables, I told her — 'Not for me. I'm not hungry.'

'Why are you not hungry? You had nothing after coffee. No. No. Take dinner.' Madam insisted.

'Sorry darling. Not today.' And I left for bedroom. Madam followed me finding me extremely morose.'

'Unless you share your grief with me, how can I do anything. After all, I am your wife and you can share your problem whatever it is. Please, for God sake, Pritesh, be frank as you usually are. I won't be able to tolerate your silence and lack of hunger. Please Pritesh.'

She took my left hand in her hand and put right hand round my neck. She didn't kiss me and insisted again. I had to narrate what had happened in Panipat and how Toshi was being blamed for murder of seven vagabonds. That made her serious and thoughtful. She consoled me saying — 'Look Pritesh. We ought to talk to Toshi and find out the reality behind these cases. If she has done all this, which I don't expect from a homely girl, then we take the help of Sarpanch who has good relations with a large number of police inspectors and promoted Kotwals. But maybe she is innocent, then money will solve the problem. Money makes the mare go.'

'I fail to decide how to proceed further. Helpless as I am, I am unable to take any action.' I told her with my hand on her thigh.

'But you have to take no action. We ought to be defensive in such situation. The criminal lawyer and the police will be contacted for safety of Toshi and parents.' she suggested.

Next minute the call bell rang and I saw my parents and sister Toshi standing at the gate in C.C.T.V. camera screen. I was further shocked and expected some more tragic news. Brother didn't come and rang me up. I asked madam to wear-blouse and put on Bindi on her face. She asked the maid to prepare tea and snacks and then dinner for three more people.

I welcomed my parents at the threshold of this bungalow and touched their feet. I shook hand with my sister and patted her shoulder. Since they had felt a lot of anguish, they had fake smile on their faces. Yet I hugged my mother for the first time and had tears in my eyes. I felt sorry for not visiting home for nearly four months.

I asked them to feel comfortable in the drawing room and they felt surprised seeing the furniture, wall pictures and A.C. there. Madam herself brought water and tea in the tray and touched their feet. Mother and father looked at me with a surprise and before any bad thing could happen I confessed — 'She is Shraddha, my dear wife. Sorry for not taking your permission. Things happened in a hurry and we had no time for visiting Panipat. We had planned to see all of you after Diwali. It is good that you are here. Welcome home.'

As Shraddha had dared to touch their feet, my parents blessed her thinking — Done is done and it can't be undone at all. Moreover, they had been in a pitiable situation already since last two weeks, they didn't think it proper to aggravate their sufferings.

My mummy simply told Shraddha — 'Sorry, Bahu. Had we known about this wedding, we would have come with a gift for you. But your gift is due towards us.'

'Doesn't matter mummy ji. Your sweet words are a real gift for me. My utmost pleasure is that I got your blessings.'

Mummy added — 'May you be ever prosperous and happy. Our blessings for both of you. Pritesh must have told you all about us. Nothing to hide.'

'It is O.K.'

Papa narrated the situations as he never hoped shooting of seven people from Toshi. She had no personal pistol though the police inspectors had taken thorough search of his apartments twice. Yet Toshi was their target.

Papa told me that the local M.L.A. Mr. Gill supported them and had spoken to the S.P. that girls are to be defended in every situation. Actually, there was terrible political rivalry between Reeva and M.L.A. as the former had contested last assembly election against him and lost the election by a low margin. Secondly, Reeva was expected to contest the next assembly election against him. At least M.L.A. was happy with the murder of Reeva though a few constables doubted his role in the murder of Reeva.

Vikram had stayed with my family in these critical days and supported Toshi due to his friendship with Ajoy. He succeeded in getting the whole market closed to protest against police doubts — 'Can't girls learn shooting with guns? How could a homely girl kill seven rascals?

Was police unhappy with the murder of kidnappers, pimps and chauth takers? The Kotwal had been threatened of students' agitation if Toshi was further questioned. He told him — It is open secret that the constables take bribes from drug dealers, gamblers, prostitutes and other anti-social elements. All this must stop. Remember sir, if innocent girls are harassed by police, the citizens can retaliate.'

Out of anger Kotwal asked — 'What do you mean with 'retaliate?'

'Better you consult the dictionary for that.' And the contingent left the police station.

Madam asked mummy not to be afraid of this situation as she used to say — The worst could happen even after that or a lot of misfortunes happen in life though we never expect them. Man is enigmatic and flexible like anything. Two hours ago we were happy and she had been busy with business affair.

She told mummy — 'You don't worry now. Take dinner first.'

'We are not hungry.' Papa replied roughly.

'Why not hungry? This is dinner time and you all in your son's home. Don't you feel so?'

They kept mum.

Chanchal said — 'Namastey.'

And then offered food in the drawing room itself. I enjoyed dinner with family and felt — What is the pleasure of taking dinner with parents, sister and wife.'

After dinner, parents and Toshi were asked to relax in the newly prepared bedroom and one more bed was added by Chanchal. Madam wanted to press the legs of my mummy but she refused saying — 'Am I that old, Bahu?'

But I pressed the legs of my father after a gap of four months and he felt delighted telling my mummy — 'Look, my son has not changed in Ambala. How happy I feel.' After fifteen minutes or so I came to my bedroom where Toshi had talked about her present tensions with madam. She wanted to be police officer like Madam Kiran Bedi and not a killer like Phoolan Devi. Of course, she made forecast that she would take revenge from present police officers after she qualifies for police job. She had shown the paper cutting of column written on Defence of Women by Kamala Nain. And she left to sleep in another room.

20

After Toshi had left I thought of her life and realized that life was pretty complex and difficult to face. On the contrary, I had found life easy and comfortable in the last five days, playing badminton, kissing rosy cheeks of madam, getting money transferred in my name and then planning for blanket trading.

Madam asked me — 'Pritesh, don't get worried too much. Do you know — worrying is like joining one's own funeral procession? It is just our beginning of married life and I stand with you all the way, through every thick and thin. Have patience darling because we can plan for solution in moments of cool-headedness. Feel happy if Toshi could kill seven rascals. But that is all yesterday as pistol is a mystery. Police officers want to find out the pistol first. Only then process of investigation will start. I'll call Sarpanch and he'll talk with City Kotwal here. These officers are interconnected due to transfers and often blood relations or friendly relations.'

'I am thinking of tomorrow. What'll happen if the police inspector reaches here chasing her.'

'No problem. I'll face them. Maybe some other rascals of Panipat are having gang war as happens in major towns. After all, we have to survive in this world as it is and take precaution at the same time. Leave thinking too much as you are supposed to analyze the main issues —

Was Toshi really kidnapped by Bhandari?

Did she really kill his helpers next day?

Where is her pistol if at all she carries a pistol?

Unless proof is confirmed in the law court, she has a chance to get benefit of doubt.

Even if all these murders have been committed, though I fail to accept this, we have to support Toshi. Legal cases take years in court and witness counts in the court. Mostly the police officers lose the cases without proper witness and clear method of presentation. It's not a day's job — 'justice hurried is justice buried' is a famous saying. If police produces fake witnesses, we can do the same with money. After all, she is Under Officer in N.C.C. and I'll seek the help of Tiwari uncle. Secondly, she may be advised to join Arya College Ambala as she is the champion in basketball and football. Due to her height she has bright future in Defence.'

'That's alright.'

'Fine. Then try to sleep.' She took me to her heart and kissed me. I felt a little relieved and yet pitied my miserable parents. Of course, I was still afraid of the fact — What'll happen if she has been the killer in these three incidents.'

After Toshi and parents left Panipat by 5.30 P.M., two brothel keepers were killed at 5.15 P.M. And next morning's newspaper gave the news. Again, the Kotwal doubted Toshi's role and reached Ajoy's home and shop. When they were told of the visit of parents with Toshi to Ambala round 5.15 P.M., they searched the footage at bus station and saw three of them entering the bus for Ambala at 5.30 P.M. Still they took my address and made us awake to check the footage of my C.C.T.V. camera of the last ten days. Here they found that my parents and Toshi reached this bungalow only after 8 P.M. This made them thoughtful and one inspector told the another one that Toshi may not have any role in any murder whatsoever.

But law and order situation worsened in Panipat and two gamblers killed two constables when the latter raided their gambling centre. Next day there was gang war among four boot-leggers and they killed each other. S.S.P. Karnal took serious action immediately and transferred the whole police officers except the record keeper from Panipat Kotwali.

Reading all these news Toshi made a phone call to L.I.U. Inspector — 'Hello, Sir. Who is behind this new violence? Will you blame Toshi for managing gambling and boot-legging? Always remember sir, Victimizers often become victims. This is the working of Fate, unknown in your dictionary, perhaps. Bye.'

As my parents wanted to leave for Panipat after lunch, madam requested them politely to stay — 'Is this not your home Papa, Mummy? Since Pritesh is your son, you have to stay a week or so. I have not shown you my house and the opening ceremony will take place day after tomorrow. Your blessings and Didi Toshi's presence matters a lot for both of us. Please Papa.'

Papa looked towards mummy and Toshi and they told her — 'But we didn't carry many clothes. Next time we'll stay for a week definitely Bahu Rani. Let us go now.' Papa pleaded.

'Clothes will be arranged within an hour for three of you. I have to go to the market for shopping for the ceremony. Mummy and Didi can accompany me and buy what is needed. Most important factor is that some clothes are offered by bride's parents to the parents, brothers and sisters of bridegroom. That'll be done today as I have no father to buy the same. Pritesh, why don't you force your parents to stay?'

'Yes. Papa, mummy. Madam is totally justified. Now, stay for her sake if not for me.' I politely said. They remained silent and madam asked the maid to prepare tea for them too.

Tomorrow and Tomorrow and Tomorrow

Then we took Papa, mummy and Toshi to the salesroom, store room and showed them the blankets, lohis, shawls etc. that we had bought. She asked Papa to select a blanket of his choice and mummy to select a shawl for herself. They felt pleased with these two gifts.

I asked Toshi — 'If you have any liking for shawl, you may have one. But she had made up her mind to buy a pair of jeans, two T-Shirts and a Jacket.

I didn't know what my parents felt with my marriage but accepted each request of madam. She was so humble to them as she had spoken the word 'Papa' after twenty years. She could talk to my mummy though her mummy could not, yet she took my parents to the room of her mummy and tried to explain her marriage with me with her Bindi. As a result, her mummy hinted towards her pillow from where madam took five notes of denomination of 2000 and gave two notes to Papa, one to mummy, one to Toshi and finally last one to me. I resisted but then madam added — 'This is a gift and both of us will enjoy ice-cream with it.'

After breakfast mummy asked madam — 'Bahu, did you both visit Shiva's Temple as couple just after marriage celebration?'

Madam felt sorry and lamented — 'There was none to guide both of us. I have never been taught that way. Yet it is never late to visit the temple. Since all of you are here, we both go to temple to seek blessings of Lord Shiva in the temple. Of course, we light the lamp before Lord Shiva and Lord Krishna every morning without fail. This I learnt from my Papa too. Once we went to the temple on way to Ludhiana. Today we offer Thali and coconut before the Lords. What else is required mummy?'

'Let's us reach there first and there I'll take care of other things.'

We reached Lord Shiva Temple within fifteen minutes and Thali full of flowers was bought with a coconut and oil lamp.

Some fruits and sweets had been carried by mummy from the kitchen. Pandit ji blessed us both and the Thali was offered to the Lords. Mother donated hundred rupees in the donation box and gave another hundred rupees to Pandit ji. As there were not many devotees in the temple, mummy asked Pandit ji to guide the newly married couple. Soon he was ready and we sat on the floor near the gate and he told us the gist of *The Bhagwadgita* briefly —

(a) Negative thinking is responsible for our fall.

(b) Right knowledge solves our daily problems.

(c) Selflessness ultimately leads to prosperity and peace.

(d) Prayers give solace to inner heart and sub-conscious mind.

(e) Give up personal pride and accept blissful ways as taught by Lord Krishna to Arjuna.

(f) Get connected with soul-consciousness daily.

(g) Learn moral lessons from what you study from epics and shastras.

(h) Don't leave interest in your real self.

(i) Attach importance to the blessings of Gods and parents and good wishes of friends.

We thanked him for this blessings and touched the feet of Pandit ji and parents and left the temple with Prasad. I hinted madam — this is the advantage of elderly people in the family.

Since madam always carried her credit card she required mummy to visit the Mall from where I had bought a few clothes for myself. She bought two synthetic sarees for my mummy, four readymade shirts for my papa and two jeans and two t-shirts for my sister. Then I naturally asked her to buy something for herself and she selected two silk sarees on the suggestion of mummy. Then we enjoyed ice-cream in the ice-cream parlour and felt happy.

21

In these two days Toshi became intimate with Chanchal and helped her in the kitchen as she used to assist mummy in Panipat. As both of them were students of B.A. Part I, they shared their thoughts with each other on political and economic issues. Of course, they did gossip about film heroes and heroines. Like Toshi, Chanchal had a desire to study *Western Thought* and Toshi told her the name of book written by Dr. Ramesh Mohan on this subject. As she had to miss her regular classes, she wished to hire a teacher for an hour who could teach her English Literature. She had taken madam's permission as she herself was almost free after lunch and dishwashing. Her mother had promised to pay the fees of her coaching if somebody was ready to help her in the bungalow.

On her genuine request I contacted my friend Ashok Gill to teach her @ of two thousand rupees per month. Next day was a new day for Toshi as well as Chanchal as smart Ashok came to teach them. On my request he had two copies of the book on *English Poetry* and his pronunciation won their heart. Their coaching removed the tension of maid Dhania.

There was a sudden change in the mind of Toshi as she felt tense these days for being questioned by the police. She thought it best to stay with me and get her admission transferred from Arya College, Panipat to Arya College, Ambala. The new principal felt impressed with her performance in basket-ball, volley-ball and foot-ball. Of course, Toshi was not ready to give up the rank of Under Officer of N.C.C. The principal assured her to find out the way for that. Madam welcomed her and asked her to live in the bedroom that we had just left.

Chanchal and Toshi started playing billiards and Toshi's game tricks were admired by madam. Actually, Toshi had played billiards with Dipali in her Kothi at Panipat. The principal of Arya College, Panipat felt happy issuing her the transfer certificate but hesitated putting signature on her character certificate. But Toshi told him politely — 'Sir, do you regard your daughter a killer of vagabonds? Nearly eight anti-social elements have been killed after my departure. Don't you wish to encourage the girls who face kidnappers of girls?'

'O.K. Beta. My good wishes for your future.' And he put his signature on character certificate too.

It was God-gift to her to remember what she heard once. Since she spoke in English with police inspector and Kotwal, they failed to face her in high volume. Her reasons were logical as there was no evidence against her — No F.I.R. and no witness.

She rarely attended the periods of History and Economics here. But she started preparing for training for Lieutenant's post. Being pretty smart, bold and courageous, she became intimate with many girls. Once she took part in the army parade and left a deep impression upon the Brigadier with shooting ten out of ten. That boosted her morale and she was properly awarded a coat with army logo. The Brigadier asked her to join Army as shooters were urgently required on Kashmir border to face the terrorists. Within next two weeks she got temporary appointment and felt tension free.

Fortunately or unfortunately the same L.I.U. Inspector and sub-inspector Sukhveer Singh got transferred to Ambala Police Station. When she reached the Police Station for routine character verification, these two tried to create hurdles in her way. But Toshi was no ordinary girl and she told the Kotwal — 'They are unhappy with me because I took their pictures taking bribes from criminals. I can show the same to you sir.'

Within seconds both her opponents left Kotwal's office. She told the Kotwal — 'An officer is honest unless his video is uploaded and then made viral.'

'Yes, yes, I understand and signed the document. With the help of Sarpanch she found out the legal custodian of that stolen pistol.

She wanted to return it to the rightful owner. After checking the details on the internet, she noticed that some Vishal Ladhu of Karnal was its owner. By chance Vishal Ladhu was earning money from his rice mill. She contacted him on phone, much against the will of her group of Kammo and Shanu and Lahiri Ladhu responded.'

'Who are you? What do you want?'

'I am a student of Arya College. Will you please tell if Vishal Ladhu's pistol was stolen?'

'Yes. It was with your voice I guess that I am talking to my classmate Toshi with whom I studied in Jain College, Panipat.'

Toshi felt surprised and had to accept.

'But Lahiri, you have to pay one lac rupees cash in case you need the pistol.'

'Well Toshi. That's no problem. I am in Karnal at the moment and reach you after an hour.'

After an hour Lahiri met Toshi with one lac rupees and she handed over the pistol to him asking him to promise — 'Don't tell anybody about me. This is a serious matter.'

'Yes. I know. There are many killings in Panipat these days.'

As he offered her coffee and cakes, he tried to be friendly with her and felt tempted to kiss her. With her judo trick she overpowered him and warned — 'No kidding Lahiri. Take your way and leave. I am no ordinary girl — I am Toshi — a girl like Kiran Bedi.'

Presence of parents and Toshi was a delight for both of us and Singhal had been entrusted the job of inauguration ceremony. Aluminum gates and windows had been installed. The rooms glittered as the interior decorator had done the needful. Women shawls and small pieces of blankets were displayed with necessary details. The elevator had started working and added to our comfort.

The Brigadier reached the bungalow in time and inaugurated the showroom with clappings from all and madam showed him the items that we intended to trade with. It was no occasion for any speeches and he wished good luck to madam and me for all success.

He admired one A grade blanket and one shawl A grade for his wife and insisted to pay saying — 'Gifts are given to daughters. You are like my daughter and hence can't accept gifts from you. Your bunch of flowers is enough. I'll leave just after coffee as I told you.' And he really left by his green car soon.

Dipali, close friend of Yukti, had come with her grandeur and expressed her interest in our items. She bought two A grade pink blankets, one shawl for her mother and one for herself. But then she asked madam — 'Excuse me, Can we easily get men's shawls stiched as men shirts?'

'Yes, of course. In winters it'll be comfortable.' Madam told her.

Then Dipali bought twenty almond shade shawls for her servants of Panipat. She offered a cheque and then enjoyed coffee with Yukti and madam.

These days Naini's Papa had been out of job as some bungling was traced out by the officer. She had fallen on terrible days and couldn't pay the second instalment of college fee. On the request of Yukti, she was offered a job as a sales girl. Salary for her was to be told after a week after seeing her performance.

Yukti bought one blanket of A grade, one shawl for her father and another for her mother. Forty blankets of A grade were bought by different members of Ambala Club, well known to madam. Police Kotwal bought one blanket and left after taking coffee.

While sipping her coffee madam got a call from Brigadier Tiwari — 'If you can supply five thousand woollen dark green shirts within fifteen days, let me know. After this supply I order you for another fifteen thousand shirts.'

He gave one phone number of his assistant officer to know further details.

Madam discussed the issue with me as if we were losing our track. But the request of Tiwari ji could not be turned down. Hence, madam contacted his assistant officer and got all details on e-mail. As a result, she contacted a contractor of Ambala who used to supply a lot of things in bulk. He was ready to do the needful within limited period but charged rupees ten extra per shirt. Madam thought it better to adjust.

On-line supply of items was to be looked after by Naini and billing was to be done carefully. She was asked to take help from Mr. Singhal if needed. However, we two could be consulted.

Tomorrow is not tomorrow if it does not bring new news or new events don't happen. New thoughts, good or bad, logical or irrational do come to one's mind next day. And madam noticed on the third day that she had missed her monthly period. She didn't share it with me and yet became conscious of the fact — There was beginning of new life for her. She recollected the sound she had heard of 'Maa'. The baby was supposed to come out of her womb to call her Maa and me as Papa.

My parents and Toshi's pleasure knew no bounds when madam told us of this development. After all, woman is the creator and mother of the whole mankind. No woman — no child. I hoped that with this she would forget the memories of her first marriage as human mind is aptly regarded most flexible.

◘

22

My Papa told me about the rivalry between Lala Karam Chand Jain and Lala Mohan Das Jain on the purchase of a piece of land of three hundred yards adjoining the Jain Temple in Jain Street.

Both of them were dedicated devotees of Lord Mahaveer and offered morning prayers in the temple. Both of them aspired to live in the house adjoining the temple even in old age. They wished to die listening the temple bells.

Lala Karam Chand's son managed to buy that piece of land paying five lac rupees more to the seller and within six months built a nice house of two floors. There was no limit to Lala Karam Chand's joy now as he could easily visit the temple even being pretty old. The servant was to accompany him and after he had offered the prayers, gave him the rosary to count the beads.

Unfortunately Lala Karam Chand had failed to marry a very beautiful girl of Gannaur though the proposal for her came for him first.

Since Lala Karam Chand's father was greedy and demanded huge dowry from the girl Padma's father and the marriage could not be solemnized. But then Lala Mohan Das came to know about the grand face and other features of Padma from neighbouring women. Through his cashier he sent his proposal for the hand of Padma and won the queen for himself. He didn't bother for money and felt that a beautiful girl is dowry in itself as she becomes the mother of his pretty children.

From Padma Lala Mohan Das got two sons and a daughter and all of them were pretty. Lala ji earned good amount of money in Reliance shares and then with stock of gold. He purchased gold @ of ten thousand rupees per ten grams and sold it @ of rupees fifty thousand rupees per ten grams.

After the construction of Lala Karam Chand's house, an old house just in the south of temple was for sale for rupees twenty lacs and elder son of Mohan Das bought that, demolished and constructed a better house than the rival of his father. From here Lala Mohan Das could see the large statue of Lord Mahaveer and Lord Bahubali and also hear the temple bells. Like any Christian, Lala ji felt delight whenever he heard the ringing of bells in the temple. But somehow he felt that bells call for him. Maybe the time had come for him to depart. Since he had no serious illness, though aged fifty eight, his sons asked him not to think of death.

Pretty daughter of Lala Mohan Das studied in Kurukshetra University, Haryana in M.B.A. and started loving Lala Karam Chand's second son Praneet as he was her classmate. Since both of them were from well-off families, they bunked classes and enjoyed love-making in Manali, Shimla, Solan, Dalhousie etc. Tammannah was young (20), pretty witty and first rank player of tennis and billiards. Praneet played tennis against her in the matches and finally won her heart. They enjoyed singing and dancing and hence had physical relations. One of the friends of her father Sumit had seen them together in a hotel dancing on Rock Music. And that day onwards, Tammannah had rough times. Lala Karam Chand's son was mad for Tammannah and threatened his father of suicide if he failed to get Tammannah.

Lala Mohan Das's son had to compromise and manage his sister's marriage with Praneet with a heavy heart. Lala Mohan Das no more boasted of his wife's beauty before everybody as traditional people often told him — 'Lala ji, you failed to control your daughter.'

But Tammannah didn't bother for the pseudo-pride of her father and departed to Praneet's home, just nearby. After a year she got a pretty son called him Pappey.

Son of Lala Mohan Das got a new hall constructed in Jain Dharamshala in the name of his father spending roughly fifteen lac rupees. Again it irked Lala Karam Chand but the situation had changed. Due to the marriage of Tammannah and Praneet, both the families forgot their former enmity and felt forced to accept each other's expectations.

Even in her middle age Padma had maintained her figure and Lala Karam Chand stealthily looked towards her in functions. Yet he failed to express his regrets for demanding dowry and still aspired to have her in his arms.

And Padma always felt jealous of him as she had been neglected by Lala Karam Chand. She expected to be approved by the first young guy that reached her house for marriage.

Till fate united her with Lala Mohan Das, she felt regular grief — How did he dare to ignore her? She shared her grief with her mother and latter told her — 'Greed is the father of sin.'

And after marriage with Mohan Das, she requested him to get this sentence painted on the outer wall of new house. It was a bitter remark against Lala Karam Chand and he had to pocket the insult. Openly he urinated on this wall in late hours. But the slogan was again painted on every Dipawali.

The people of the street failed to understand and realize the word

G

R

E

E

D

that Lala Mohan Das asserted with the slogan. But the elderly people knew its implications. I asked Papa — 'Is that sentence still painted on the outer wall of Lala Mohan Das?'

Papa told me — 'It was not after the love union of Tammannah and Praneet.'

Of course, Padma was reluctant to arrange the marriage of her daughter with Praneet telling her — 'They are greedy people, Beti.'

'No, mummy, Praneet is well-off, well-educated, a smart player and does not mind spending money. I know for sure.'

'Still I doubt if he is that liberal in matters of money. You never know about men — when do they change emotionally like weather?'

But Tammannah's stubbornness made her melt. Still she felt afraid of Lala Karam Chand and didn't appear alone in his presence. She entertained Praneet as worthy mother-in-law and bought costly gifts for son-in-law and her daughter and not for Lala Karam Chand.

Lala ji tolerated all this as his son had won the heart of Padma's daughter and hoped that his grandchildren, if not children, will have the blood and genes of Padma.

Secondly, Lala Mohan Das had forgotten the remark on greed. Whenever Lala Karam Chand visited Lala Mohan Das, he took his wife with himself though unconsciously noticed the wide difference between Padma and his wife.

Fate had played two games — first, it checked the union of Karam Chand and Padma. But then fate made amendment and united Padma's daughter with Praneet. Are we not just puppets in the hands of Immanent Will?

My parents left for Panipat just a week before Dipawali though both of us requested them humbly to celebrate the festival with us. On the contrary, my mummy asked madam and me — 'Bride celebrates her first Dipawali with in-laws. You both come to Panipat to join us and enjoy. My other three children will feel happy meeting you.'

But madam pretended that a lot of gifts have got to be gifted to several people and hence she'll join them next year. It was however agreed between us that we soon will visit Panipat. Somehow my mummy liked the features and conduct of Naini and considered her a suitable match for my younger brother without bothering for her present penury. Madam took this responsibility and asked my mummy to send the picture of my younger brother.

Toshi was supposed this afternoon to leave for her short training in I.M.A. Dehradun and from there take a flight for Jammu and Kashmir. Madam gifted her a smart phone and asked her to keep in touch and concentrate upon job. She felt happy with madam but Chanchal found herself lonely with Toshi's sudden departure. She had planned to pass B.A. in her company but alas! Drops had to go in different directions. However, Toshi referred the names of Kammo and Shanu to Lahiri Ladhu and told him — 'Kammo is amorous and suitable for you. She is emotional and maybe you prefer her to me. But don't ignore, Shanu as they behave like twins.'

As a result, the love story of Kammo and Ladhu developed shortly and he visited them in Panipat and entertained them in hotel Sunny Dreams. Kammo felt attracted towards Ladhu as he was a rich guy, smart, well-dressed, soft-spoken, a law graduate from Chandigarh University, owned Honda City and spent money lavishly. Soon Kammo and Shanu got their names transferred to Karnal Khalsa College and applied for pistol for each. Ladhu financed them and bribed the Arms' clerk to get the licence. Since kidnapping had become a problem, the pistol helped these girls regain their confidence.

After getting pistols they kidnapped the Income Tax Officer who had troubled Ladhu and demanded five lac rupees as bribe to get his case settled from Bengluru Income Tax Office. As Ladhu was not prepared to part this money, the officer was shot dead while coming from his office. After two days the Head Clerk of G.S.T. was shot in the office chair itself in his cabin.

Kammo and Shanu enjoyed Bohemian life with two male friends of Ladhu in his farmhouse without expecting any police action. But then all of them were playing with

F

I

R

E

and risk was not estimated, analyzed and assessed. Foolish and impractical as they were.'

◻

23

Diwali is one of the loving festivals in India and all sections of society celebrate it with vigour and enthusiasm. I used to enjoy Diwali celebration with my parents though it was the simplest way — One packet of candles, old clay lamps, kheel and half kilogram sweets. Maybe my younger brother aspired to celebrate Diwali this time with new grandeur as he had a wide circle of friends. I sent S.M.S. to Kammo and Shanu on this occasion and madam also sent more than 100 S.M.S. on this occasion to members of Ambala Club, Brigadier Tiwari and Ambala Brigadier, City Kotwal etc.

On Dhanteras she told me to plan to visit her farm and see the development of village school. Since the Sarpanch had not joined the opening ceremony, madam took a Lohi for him as Diwali gift.

After breakfast I saw that she dressed herself in pink saree and blouse (Rajasthani type) and then we left for the village. On the way she bought ten kilogram apples for the orphans and distributed them among the children of orphanage. The construction of rooms had started and was likely to be completed as per schedule.

It was my first visit to her farm and farmhouse. She stopped at the gate of Sarpanch's house and was told by his wife that he had been ill for some days. I accompanied madam and took the packet of sweets and the Lohi to be gifted and saw the Sarpanch. However, they both talked of the progress of construction of village school. His wife offered tea to both of us and it was milky tea in the sense that it had been prepared only with milk. Madam failed to touch any of the cookies that were served. Sarpanch told her that he will visit the showroom with his wife as he gets well.

The guard of the farm was asked to clean the farmhouse and then madam and I inspected the fields full of sugarcanes. She felt delighted with the crop and a few furrows were full of flowers. Here madam had maintained three buffaloes and there was a permanent attendant to look after them. Forage was grown on the farm itself and the waste of mustard plants was offered after taking out the oil. Of course, 3/4 oil was sold in the market. A part of it was later on sent to orphans for preparing their food etc.

She asked the guard to change the water of the small swimming pool and in the meantime we relaxed a little in the farmhouse. Now madam discussed her new project to establish a Milk Dairy with fifteen New Jersey Cows and had asked the attendant to find out another attendant to assist him. As a matter of fact, she had studied a book of Dairy Management and was ready to buy one New Jersey Cow @ of four lac rupees each.

I just advised — 'Why to get extra busy madam?'

She told me — 'The guard does not run the train, he looks after the system.'

I got the hint and kept silent.

We made love in the new situation after enjoying swimming in that pond and felt delighted. It was pleasant to be with her in water though she entered water in blouse and skirt. The guard had been asked to shut the door of the gate and stand there to check the entry of any unwanted person. Yet we entered the farmhouse to make love.

Madam found herself close to nature and explained to me the names of a few flowers that blossomed there. It was the duty of the attendant to bring three kilogram milk and flowers to the bungalow every morning and a bike had been given to him for this. Now onwards he was to send five kilogram milk for the orphans.

I told madam — 'You look gorgeous in every dress.'

'That's an old compliment from you. Is there nothing new?'

'Yes. The more I love you, the more passionate I feel. Why does this hunger not subside?'

'Let the flame of love ever burn dear. Don't extinguish it. If there is no love between us, life will become unbearable.'

Then she asked me to light a lamp before Maa Kali as there was a picture of the goddess in the drawing room. When she recited the poem of Vivekananda she appeared to be a perfect poet :

> ...
>
> Misery in his cup of happiness,
> Deadly venom in his drink of nectar,
> Poison in his throat — yet he clings to hope!
> Lo! how all are scared by the Terrific,
> None seek Elokeshi whose form is Death.
> The deadly frightful sword, reeking with blood,
> They take from Her hand, and put a lute
> Instead!
> Thou dreaded Kali the All-destroyer,
> Thou alone art true; Thy shadow's shadow
> Is indeed the pleasant Vanamali.
> O Terrible Mother, cut quick the core,
> Illusion dispel — the dream of happiness,
> Rend asunder the fondness for the flesh.

"It is the demons that the Mother kills!"
They only pretend they wish to see Thee,
But when the time comes, at Thy sight they
flee.
Thou art Death! To each and all in the world
Thou distributest the plague and disease
— Vessels of venom filled by Thine own hands.

After that she asked the guard to distribute Prasad among the labourers working in the fields and on the site of school building. Since she relaxed and thought of Vivekananda, she recited another poem of the prophet :

> The stars are blotted out,
>   The clouds are covering clouds,
> It is darkness vibrant, sonant.
>   In the roaring, whirling wind
> Are the souls of a million lunatics
>   Just loose from the prison-house,
> Wrenching trees by the roots,
>   Sweeping all from the path.
> The sea has joined the fray,
>   And swirls up mountain-waves,
> To reach the pitchy sky.
>   The flash of lurid light
> Reveals on every side
>   A thousand, thousand shades
> Of Death begrimed and black —
>   Scattering plagues and sorrows,
> Dancing mad with joy,
>   Come, Mother, come!
> For Terror is Thy name,
>   Death is in Thy breath,
> And every shaking step
>   Destroys a world for e'er.
> Thou 'Time', the All-Destroyer!

Come, O Mother, come!
Who dares misery love,
    And hug the form of Death,
Dance in Destruction's dance,
    To him the Mother comes.
                    (*Kali the Mother*)

I got spiritual pleasure when I heard her recitation. Earlier I had never heard such recitation of English poem though my friends told me that (Dr. Raja Karam Singh also recites the poems of Vivekananda spontaneously as if he was poet himself.) When I clapped to admire her sweet voice, she told me — 'You've not yet seen my wholeself. Have you?'

'Yes. I feel surprised with your positive attitude towards life.' And kissed her. But she tightly embraced me saying 'thanks' for admiring and listening the poems of the saint.

She added — 'Very rare people read the poems of this saint. Perhaps you may not be knowing that Roman Rolland wrote a grand book on Swami Ramkrishna Paramhansa and Vivekananda which I have failed to follow the whole on Hindu philosophy.'

'Yet it is superb to have that book at least you tried to follow it. There are scholars who have not even seen this book.' I remarked.

'I'll give you to read it and then we discuss its fundamentals with each other.' She suggested.

Diwali preparations were being made in this village too. I noticed that Haryana villages were well-connected with the towns and there was electric supply in each house. Farmers were well-built and hard-working. Hospitals had been built there to take care of the health of farmers and their families. They sent their sons and daughters to hostels to get college education. Some of them had heard of the atrocities of partition and hence knew the value of basic and higher education. Insurance schemes of L.I.C. were known to them. More than 50% of farmers had tractors and tubewells and utilized credit card facilities. As they heard T.V. news almost daily, they knew about the new welfare schemes of the government. Of course, they tried to compete with the farmers of Punjab but could not. Unfortunately, some of them had become addicted to drugs and consumption of wine had increased there. Yet half of R.N. Tagore's hope for free India got fulfilled by now.

After enjoying packed lunch, we rested in the farmhouse as madam felt a little drowsy. While lying by my side, she asked — 'Will you continue to loving me after I have a child?'

'Definitely. The child is supposed to be a link between us. After all, ours is a natural love and unplanned.'

She kissed me, took me in her arms and slept.

◻

24

Next tomorrow gave me the greatest surprise of my life. Since I slept late last night, I got up a bit late. When I opened my eyes, I heard madam talking to somebody in the drawing room. Within minutes she asked Dhania to prepare tea and ask me to join her. I had tea there and recognized advocate Sharma ji and saw some bond papers (old and new) lying on the table. Without any discussion before this morning, madam never told me about the steps that she was taking. She had asked the advocate to prepare her will transferring all her assets — the hostel building, the two farms, farmhouse, this bungalow, her ornaments and cash money nearly three crores in my name.

Even in the presence of Sharma ji I asked her to postpone this preparation of

W

I

L

L

at the moment and think again. But she was adamant and asked me to wait and watch. After departure of Sharma ji, she told me — 'I have seen three deaths so far and you know the tragic death of Mirdul. Any damn thing can happen with your wife madam too. Don't you know about the word KAAL which does not forecast its working. At the moment I am hale and hearty and you're with me round the clock. But then I don't wish any controversy about my assets after my sudden departure. Don't regard it as my hasty step. You'll realize its validity in any unexpected event.'

I had to keep mum. Then she proposed — 'You get yourself insured for one crore rupees with L.I.C. immediately so that you may have a regular income in hard times. Secondly, the agent will be selling mediclaim policy of one crore for both of us and we are supposed to pay fifty thousand rupees a year. Keep a diary for their records. I'll manage a leather bag to keep documents safe.' She assured me.

But then I took her hands in mine and told her — 'You are with me as force behind the force.'

I asked — 'Has someone threatened you recently?'

'No. Both of the sons of Smt. Indira Gandhi got killed unexpectedly. We may be targeted any time as the crime rate is increasing in almost the whole of Northern India. You read news of violence, kidnapping, abduction, theft, threats etc. daily. So safety first, speed afterwards.'

'O.K. But this will?'

'Yes. You will know that I am pregnant. My child should get all the pleasures and physical comforts that I have enjoyed so far. Don't think I am dying tomorrow or day after tomorrow. Only safety measures have been taken with minor expenses. Is it O.K.?' Sharma ji left with our signature on documents.

To assure me of her sincerity she came closer to me and kissed me on my cheeks. We embraced each other in the drawing room and shut the door. As usual we offered our love to each other and loved as Vulcan might have loved Venus in the absence of Mars, her husband. Mars got an invisible net prepared to catch Vulcan and Venus making love with each other. Yet Venus didn't stop loving Vulcan and was ready to die for her lover. If a woman's passion is above fear and earthly limitations, it is not surprising. Critics feel surprised with the fact that Venus regarded Vulcan superior to Roman God Mars. God really reveals himself with our emotions and passions.

That afternoon I recollected the tragic incident which had happened with me last year on the festival of Diwali. Since I felt fed up with the sound of crackers and could not tolerate the smoke created by them, I went out of home for a stroll on Panipat — Jind Road. Here I could breathe properly and felt at ease. But within four-five minutes I noticed three young girls walking and singing on the road. One of them hinted with her finger to go to her. As I ignored her amorous call, they came to me and one of them asked — 'Didn't you notice the hint? How did you dare to ignore us?'

I kept silent. She called me 'hero' and said — 'I know how to cut down a hero to zero.'

'Still I kept quiet.'

'O.K. which hotel will you take us for fun and frolic. Young as you are, it'll be a masti tonight.' She added.

'I'm not interested in this nonsense. You are mistaken and dialing the wrong number.' I protested and yet that girl dared to kiss me passionately as she regarded me a victim for the night.

Now she searched the pockets of my pant and found no money except my ordinary handkerchief. She told her companions — 'He is penniless, good for nothing. Don't waste time with him.'

Yet she threatened — 'This road is not meant for paupers like you. People come here in the evening to have fun.'

I kept quiet and yet advanced further. After ten minutes a bike stopped by my side and the police sub-inspector was with his assistant constable. He asked me — 'What the hell are you doing here at night?'

'Nothing. I just came for a walk here to escape from pollution created by crackers.'

'Young guys enjoy crackers and you said — you hate them. Telling lies to us?'

'No. No telling lies to you sir.'

He parked the bike on his left and searched my pockets. Finding no money there he felt a little restless as he too wanted money to celebrate his Diwali. I had been regarded an easy prey but then both of them felt disappointed with my poverty. Yet he said — 'This road is not safe for students like you. Sit on my bike.'

I had no option but to follow the order. They reached the police Kotwali and asked me to sit on the bench and wait for Kotwal. After fifteen minutes or so that sub-inspector Veer Singh asked me — 'As you are a student of B.A., I give you an option. Either teach English and Social Science to my younger daughter or the case of corruption will be filed against you. Then you will have to hire an advocate and suffer for your folly. That road is defamed as Red-Light Area and walking there brings a bad name.' He suggested.

I had no choice but to accept his first proposal and gave my consent. Since my younger sister Natashi was studying in the same class, this type of forced teaching didn't hurt me much mentally. I took an oath not to go to that road even in daytime as I felt insulted with the absurd conduct of the 'bad' girls and the police. I taught these two subjects to his daughter too till 15th of July and he didn't even thank me for this.

Really poverty is a curse in itself. This was my realization. Recollection of the incident was pretty painful but then the worse could happen than this. I thanked Lord Krishna for protecting me from the defamation.

After evening coffee madam asked me to get four woollen suits stitched for myself as she had suit-length in her steel almirah. She told me with love — 'For my sake, get them stitched and always look smart, cheerful and gay. This afternoon I found you a little dull, serious and thoughtful. I purposely didn't disturb your mood as every man has his serious times. I hope you are not worried now.'

'No. Not at all. Often a few thoughts disturb me and generally I fail to ignore thoughts about my student life. Otherwise I am happy with you and enjoy the trade business. I meet the tailor that you suggest and get these suit-lengths stitched. They are really pretty. Thank you darling. I know I ought to appear smart and gay. She came close to me and kissed my neck and I responded to assure her that the clothes were superb.'

First, we offered prayers in the temple and then reached the tailor's shop to give measurement. And then she took me to a jeweller's shop and sold the gold of Mirdul for forty-nine lac rupees. Really she regarded herself and me the trustee of the amount. In her company I became conscious of the hardships of poor children, orphans, sick and old people and pitied them.

In the Mall I possessed only four hundred ten rupees that had been saved from monthly expenses. But I could buy nothing with that amount. First, madam bought six white shirts and six Zodiac ties for me and two Monte Carlo pullovers and on my request bought a cardigan for herself too. Pullovers for orphans had been ordered from some wholesale dealer.

She bought coloured candles and three silver glasses. I asked — 'Why three?'

'One for my dear Pritesh, one for my coming child and third for myself. Is it O.K.?'

'Yes. Darling O.K.'

Then she bought one chemical solution.

In the bungalow she took out silver statues of Lord Shiva, Lord Krishna, Lord Rama, Goddess Parvati, Maa Sita, Maa Radha and bronze statue of Lord Hanuman.

I felt happy seeing these statues, each one eight inches in height. She told me that her mother had bought them many years ago. Then I asked her 'Why to keep the gods under lock and key? Is it proper to shut them inside the almirah?'

'Not proper but safe. Different servants spread rumours seeing silver utensils and silver statues. For security of the family I have to do it against my own wishes,'

She convinced me and she was right. Why to display our riches? I thought. She told me that she'll herself wash the silver glasses. And at night we enjoyed champagne with them and celebrated the occasion with love.

But something unexpected and unhoped happened at night.

This night madam saw a dream and found herself serving in the Haram of Akbar The Great. As a matter of fact, no male was allowed to enter here except the Sultan as he had the liberty to enjoy sex with any of his favourites. Here madam was known as Sabeena and one night the door of her room was opened by another maid and then four maids carried her to another room outside the Haram.

She noticed to her surprise that Mirdul was one of them. She was told that Sultan desired to have her tonight. It gave her little pleasure at least she would come closer to Sultan and then would possess some powers in the Haram. But alas! She had been brought to another room where Subedar was sitting. He had formed a group of supporters in the army and also in the Haram.

The Subedar Sahib asked her — 'Do as you are ordered or else you are killed.'

'But where is Sultan Sahib?'

'Don't ask questions. Everybody is Sultan in the darkness of night.'

And then Subedar took off her Kameez and offered her a hard drink. As she resisted, he slapped her twice and again threatened to kill her. But madam cried for help — 'Help me Chanda or else I die. This is no Sultan. Even Subedar calls himself Sultan at night. Help me please, please help me. I can't surrender like this. Does Haram have no ethical code? I was told that males don't enter here. But this is totally unethical.'

Since no help came forward, the Subedar removed her salwar and entered her. She cried out of agony as she was not mentally prepared for this. It was no romance with Sultan and she was not going to be elevated there. It was disgusting to have sex with Subedar. That way she would be molested daily. No way. She cried — 'Help me, Chanda, please do something. Have I not been helpful to you so far?'

'Help me Chanda.' And she cried badly.

As I was in bed by her side, I awoke and asked her — 'What's the matter? There is no Chanda here. Who hurts you? Come out of your dream. Think of the positive side of life.'

As she opened her eyes, she found me and wept profusely. I tried to pacify her and wiped her sweating body and face. I pacified her and she told me what she had seen. These days she

often studied the book *Great Mughal Emperors* and perhaps it
was all the result of

I
M
P
R
E
S
S
I
O
N
S

that had settled in her mind.

25

As my mummy had taken the picture of Naini, she showed it to Ajoy and he approved the same saying — 'Do as you like mummy.'

However, my mummy made it clear to my Papa and Ajoy that it'll be a simple marriage without expecting anything from Naini's parents. But then Naini insisted to pass M.A. English next year as M.A. classes were supposed to start in S.D. College, Panipat in self-finance scheme. Ajoy approved her demand and promised to buy a scooty for her. But then he made it very clear to her — 'No arguments with my parents in my case' and she accepted his dictation. Of course, Naini left us one day back and in the morning of Diwali she was to wed Ajoy in the Sunny Moon Hotel.

When my mummy told me all this, we decided to join the wedding ceremony. Madam took out a ring as a gift for Naini. Now she asked me — 'Anything else sweetheart?'

I was a little emotional now and finding me sad, she asked — 'What makes you feel dull and morose?'

'Leave it.' I answered.

'Why leave it? Do you wish to present anything else to Naini? Tell me frankly.' She asked with anxiety.

'There is a problem that hurts me day and night. Madam, my father sold two gold bangles of my mother for my education in Ambala.' I sobbed.

'So?'

'I wish I could return same type of bangles to her now.'

'Only this has hurt you for weeks? Now, we buy two bangles for her today and then you'll be free from this financial burden though children are always indebted to parents. No way to get rid of their obligations. One has only one mother and one father — it is universal fact.' She replied and kissed my hand.

After buying two bangles from the jeweller, madam bought shirts, jeans, frocks etc. for my younger sister and brother.

Next tomorrow we were full of enthusiasm on account of Chhoti Diwali Celebration and Pandit ji had been requested to arrange Puja on both the evenings. Since the other staff members were on Diwali leave, madam had requested Dhania as usual to come for half a day and manage the Puja affair, lunch and dinner. A lot of crackers and flower decorations, frills of light etc. had added to the glamour of bungalow. Both of us felt delighted arranging everything. After Goddess Lakshmi Puja we touched the feet of Maa and got her blessings. She hinted madam to get two currency notes from the pillow cover and both of us thanked her for this too. I felt — I had done nothing for this noble lady. Alas! It's an unnecessary obligation. When I told this to madam, she said — 'This approach is disgusting. Had she been active, she might have done a lot for you too. A lady loves her son-in-law more than her daughter. I know her temperament, sweet as it was. Do you find her creating any panic?'

'No.'

'This confirms the patience she has.'

We finalized and checked certain bills of the last week. Of course, we were moving in the right direction. Four local shopkeepers approached madam to keep the stock of Cott's wool hosiery and they'll definitely buy in bulk from us. They said — 'You'll earn commission and we won't have to depend upon Ludhiana merchants who often misbehave due to their pride.'

Madam heard their argument, took their contact number, promised to think about it and then inform them accordingly.

It was almost daily that we had agents from woollen mills of Jalandhar, Amritsar and some villages who wished to supply blankets and shawls. Madam really failed to find out the difference between pure wool and impure. She hesitated and told them to wait as our stocks were enough at this time. We had to face a lot of journalists daily seeking advertisements of our trade. But alas!

After Puja of Lakshmi goddess, we had coffee and then enjoyed two games of billiards. We kissed each other while playing the game as we were in cotton gowns. When we returned, we were hungry. Since Dhania had prepared dinner madam did the needful in the kitchen and we dined. She switched on T.V. and I slept earlier than usual.

Since Yukti had sent Diwali greetings with S.M.S. I dreamt of her that night. So far I had never been serious about her physical charms and took her casually on account of financial gap between both of us. This night we wandered on the Mall Road of Shimla (where we had gone a year before for attending the conference), hand in hand and in an amorous mood. I kissed her shoulder as she was dressed in shoulderless top of rosy colour. Then I pressed her hips as she was looking pretty. Just she responded with a kiss on my cheek, then another cheek and then played with my hair.

She told me — 'How silly of you to have ignored my love for the sake of Madam Shraddha? I'll never forgive you to have ignored my love for the sake of madam Shraddha? I'll never forgive you for this betrayal. Now you don't take me out of hostel. All moments of fun have come to an end. We were better in Panipat where we studied jointly frequently. I could afford for your Ph.D. if you had told me.'

And then both of us were mad with love and kissed each other for more than ten minutes.

I plucked the fruit of knowledge and first gave it to her. Then she asked me to eat the same. After that we enjoyed swimming in the river Meander and had no clothes upon our body. She asked me — 'Forget madam and return to me. It is now or never. I can't wait for you any longer, for next birth.'

I kept mum but kissed her bosom passionately. She told me — 'I feel hungry now.'

I asked her to wait and plucked another apple from the same tree and offered her the same. Then we wandered freely in the garden and saw peacock, nightingale, skylark, cuckoo, swallows etc. and then she told me — 'I want to dance like a peacock and sing like a skylark? Will you manage this? For my sake, do something and I'll sing and dance before you out of my love for you.'

'O.K. Yukti. But then ...'

And I was speaking — 'But then ...', madam made me awoke and asked — 'What then sweetheart?'

'Nothing sweetheart.' I told a lie.

Tomorrow and Tomorrow and Tomorrow

26

Next tomorrow was a new day of joy in my family at Panipat as Ajoy was getting married with pretty Naini though it was a forced compromise for her. Really she wanted to take M.A. degree and then join B.Ed., then M.Ed. and then Ph.D. But alas! Her father's suspension had made her suddenly dull and morose and her mother felt forced to join a clerical job in a school.

Ups and downs are usual in everybody's life. I noticed that Ajoy and I got almost settled in life and Toshi had joined army on the basis of N.C.C. skills. Now Papa and Mummy had felt the burden of other two children only and yet hoped much from Ajoy. Papa had told Toshi to deposit some money in bank account so as to help him in arranging her marriage.

Yukti found herself alone as Kamala Nain became busier than before due to her interest in reporting news and then writing columns on socio-economic and political matters. She had a mind to join correspondence course in Mass Communication from I.G.N.O.U., New Delhi. She was writing the biography of Vivekananda.

In the beginning madam told me — 'Pritesh, if all this goes on like this, we might forget each other as we have no time for love. Often you don't remember that you got married with Shraddha.

I miss your amorous conversation and then badminton is almost forgotten. I have not worn the white kit for many days and you don't sit by my side in bed as you maintain the accounts.'

'No, sweetheart. I love you as usual.' I tried to pacify her and touched her right hand.

But she withdrew the same saying — 'This is your pretension and pseudo-love that I don't need.'

She argued with mild anger — 'How can there be

A
F
F
E
C
T
A
T
I
O
N

between you and me? I put away the computer and moved towards her to kiss. But she withdrew herself and remained silent. Eventually I rubbed her thighs and tried to excite her.

I told her — 'We go out soon to enjoy traditional life. Moreover, we have to appoint a sales girl in lieu of Naini as she will resign soon.'

'Again business issues. This is what I am complaining. Charles Lamb aptly said in the essay *The Old And The New Schoolmaster* that teacher's wife talks of the problems of students every evening with her husband and this way they forget their love for each other. She becomes children's caretaker only. Look, we discuss business affairs in future in the drawing room only and not in bedroom. Do you accept my request on love?'

'Yes. Of course, you are justified. Basically we both are inexperienced blanket dealers and have entered the market where we have a lot of competition. Anyway as you said earlier, our bread and butter never depend upon this trade.'

I continued to press her thighs and hips and she had come closer to me. We didn't sleep early as we were supposed to join the wedding ceremony of Ajoy and Naini next day. We made love and I found her almost satisfied.

Next morning we got up a bit early and left Ambala after breakfast. She dressed herself in silken saree and appeared glamorous with diamond necklace, diamond bangles and diamond rings. Before we left home, we kissed each other as I looked like Lord Mountbatten in white suit. She switched on the car music system and atmosphere was romantic.

We reached the hotel and met parents, other relations and friends like Yukti, Kamala Nain, parents of Yukti, my grandparents, uncle and aunt and some of my neighbours. All of them felt impressed with the charming figure of my wife and told my Papa that I was fortunate enough to marry Madam Shraddha.

Mummy and aunt were busy in the marriage rituals. Music was being played with music system. Madam had a desire to change her saree and I told her to wait as she already appeared captivating. My younger brothers and sister felt delighted meeting my wife. But all of us missed Toshi as she failed to get leave to join the function. Kammo and Shanu were there to meet us and told madam — 'We both will visit your bungalow to enjoy badminton and billiards.'

And madam replied with a smile — 'Of course, Didi. It'll be my pleasure to entertain you.'

Amma ji blessed both of us though I noticed her a little sad as her sons had not made progress as expected by her. To her grief they had no love like Pandavas and generally quarrelled like Kauravas. She was no more proud of her superior status as mummy had settled three of us without much trouble. Such was the working of Fate. Of course, my parents were proceeding from adversity to prosperity by the blessings of Lord Shiva, Lord Krishna and other Gods.

Often Mummy told me not to demand anything from God as He knew all our conditions, problems, obsessions and requirements and will positively help us if we do right deeds — Slow and steady wins the race. Like Virginia Woolf, my mummy was the symbol of patience and fortitude. She had loved all of us without any prejudices.

Vikrant and his wife came to us and offered good wishes for our marriage and then trade. He gave his phone number and asked me to supply him two A grade blankets through Ajoy. He invited us to visit New Delhi and stay with him in Dwarka — Really nice on his part. I reciprocated the invitation to them and felt thankful to him for helping my younger brother to settle as a jeweller without knowing the tricks that had been adopted by them both.

Kammo and Shanu introduced me to Ladhu saying — 'Our mutual friend at Karnal. He is the richest guy there as he runs rice mill.'

Smart, vigilant and clever Ladhu was dressed in white suit like me and I told madam — 'We have another Lord Mountbatten here.'

'Yes, darling. But he stands nowhere in your comparison. After all, you are the Lord of my heart.'

'Thank you madam.'

My uncle and aunt felt jealous of my parents as we got settled nicely. My grandparents blessed both of us as madam too bowed down pretending touching their feet.

Madam told me — 'Had we married in this traditional manner, I would have appeared pretty as Naini.'

'You look prettier than Naini even now. We may arrange a party sometime in December to celebrate our love — after all, we are husband and wife legally. My honeymoon fever is not over yet.'

'Really.'

'Yes, really darling!'

'I'll see to it.'

'Yes. You may.'

After ten minutes or so we entered the room as madam was eager to change her saree — ladies are extra conscious of appearing in new sarees on such occasions and it was not unusual with her. I accompanied her and after she had removed her saree and blouse to change, I caught hold of her and kissed her passionately. Then I excited her and pressed her hips and boobs and entered her.

I told her — 'This gift from Panipat Munda, darling.'

'O.K. I'll give you the return gift as Ambala Kudi soon.'

'I'll wait for you.'

But Kammo had booked another room here and made love with Ladhu.

Unfortunately, there was panic in the town as the new Kotwal had been shot in the morning on Delhi-Panipat road. As a result, the police officers took general search on the highway. I was told by Vikrant that a smart C.I.D. officer had already been sent to find out the causes of murders in Panipat and Karnal.

Naini was hugged by Yukti, Dipali, Kammo, Shanu etc. and we blessed the couple. Papa and mummy felt sad as I told them my programme to return to Ambala this evening. Out of mild anger he told me — 'You are a guest now dear son.'

'Still your son. We both will visit you probably on Bhaidooj.'

I gave him the bangles for mummy and he had tears in his eyes.

'O.K. I'll see if you fulfil this promise.'

After having lunch and blessings the couple took seven rounds of fire and we returned to Ambala. We relaxed a little and then invited Pandit ji for Lakshmi Puja. The silver statues shined in the light of candles and silver lamps. Electric frills added glamour to bungalow. Madam asked me to keep my pistol under the pillow as the guards were on leave for two days. Surprisingly, she had no sense of fear and was close to me in bed. We had sweets as a ritual and then a cup of coffee as prepared by madam. While offering coffee, she said — 'Here's your coffee my boss!' And smiled.

I remarked — 'Whenever she smiles, the world is gay!'

'Who's she now?'

'You alone darling. Who else can be another she here?'

But that night was disgusting for madam as she felt horrified in her dream.

In the dream madam saw herself behaving as old, sick and thin Aurangzeb who had killed his three brothers for the throne of whole Bharat. Actually, Sultan Shahjahan had decided to declare Dara, his eldest son, as his successor and all arrangements for Dara's coronation were being made. But Aurangzeb had mostly lived in the Deccan as its sole custodian and had killed almost all his rivals there except Shivaji Maharaj.

There was no limit to his political ambitions and hence he got his father Shahjahan Sultan arrested. In spite of his loneliness in the absence of Mumtaz, he was not easily ready to surrender his kingly powers. He had to lead a miserable life in the prison till death and son Aurangzeb had shown no sympathy for his father and latter's supporters.

Aurangzeb had ruled for more than fifty years and had destroyed many Hindu temples and idols. Yet he failed to get peace of mind and soul. Whenever he recollected his past glory, he failed to forget the cruel deeds as performed by him. He was fully conscious of his guilt and brutality and hence offering namaz appeared to be a routine.

He blamed himself as the killer of Dara who was known as a scholar of Sanskrit and Persian languages. He didn't recollect any incident when Dara or Murad had opposed him. Then why did he kill his innocent brothers? He asked himself — What is the use of this pomp and show? What has he achieved with human vanities? Do people love him or hate him? Will he be remembered for righteousness, mercy and fortitude or for brutality and cruelty? Answer was

N

E

G

A

T

I

V

E

and that further added to his dullness. His son Azam tried to know the causes of his sorrow and desperation but in vain! How could the old Sultan weep before his son? No way. After all, he was Sultan so far.

But his sorrow and grief became public when he wrote his will —

Nobody should weep on his death.

No condolence meeting be organized on his death.

No grand tomb be constructed in his memory.

His funeral ought not to be on grand scale and let him be buried in a simple manner.

Let there be no shade upon his grave.

Since he wanted to die a peaceful death, Sufi saints were asked to give him company for mental peace. But then he died a tragic death asking 'Almighty Allah to help him.'

'Ya Allah forgive me for my inhuman conduct.'

As Madam repeated this three times in dream I asked her — 'What make you seek divine mercy like this. Come to senses, please.'

And she awoke with a feeling of grief and had tears of confession. I consoled her and advised — 'Stop reading that book on Mughal Emperors please. It creates nasty thoughts in your mind.'

'O.K. Perhaps you are right.'

She took time to sleep and finally I embraced her.

27

After Bhaidooj Yukti rang me up and requested me to accompany her to Shimla to attend an International Conference on *Bolshevik Revolution And Literature*. She was quite enthusiastic about it as a few foreign delegates were expected to present their papers on various topics such as —

Bolshevik Revolution And Fall of Czar.

Bolshevik Revolution And The Failure of Lenin.

Bolshevik Revolution And Russia After 1922.

Bolshevik Revolution And George Orwell.

Bloody Revolution And Vladimir Nabokov etc.

Still I recollected that I had George Orwell's Novel *Nineteen Eighty Four* in my syllabus. But then dust had started gathering on my books and Dr. Prem Prakash felt sad when I vacated the hostel and missed the classes. When he visited our showroom, I gifted him a shawl but then he paid for the shawl selected by his worthy wife. Madam requested them to stay for dinner after they had sipped coffee. While leaving he told me — 'Pritesh, continue to read books as college authorities are not very particular about 75% attendance. Maybe you manage to pass the exam. What is the harm in getting M.A. Degree?'

I thanked him for visiting us and boosting my morale. Yet I told Yukti — 'Sorry, Yukti. It won't be possible now.'

'Why Pritesh? Won't madam allow outing with me?'

'No. It's not that. Actually, our trade is new. Secondly, I won't be able to prepare the paper these days.' I apologized.

'Yaar, we have already attended many seminars and debates in the past. Now you are a different man changed with times. How can you forget me?'

'You are feeling hurt. I know Yukti. But I'm helpless.'

Then Yukti talked to Dipali to join her company. But Dipali showed no interest in this academic programme and told her — 'At present I don't intend to attend the conference in Shimla. If at all I feel interested, I'll be there at the nick of time. Sorry Yukti.'

'It is O.K.'

Yukti found herself alone and yet prepared a paper on *Bolshevik Revolution And George Orwell's Reactions* and then sent her paper for approval along with its soft copy to the organizer. It was to be held on 7th-8th November, 2019 in the grand hall of Himachal Pradesh University. She had been looking forward to participate in International Conference and felt elevated with the approval of her paper on-line.

Yukti appeared glamorous in saree as a participant in the seminar though the people were unknown to her. It was a real pleasure for her to be among the galaxies of literature. A few participants had joined there from Russia, Ukraine, Poland, France, Germany, U.S.A., U.K. etc. and their papers were presented in the opening session just after formalities of Saraswati Vandana and garlanding the guests.

In the second session Prof. Levi of U.S.A. presided the session and Prof. Yamuna Kamal of Arya College, Ambala presented his paper on *The Influence of Bolshevik Revolution Upon Vladimir*

Nabokov. It was well admired by the listeners. After two more papers Yukti was invited to present her paper on *George Orwell And The Revolution.* As she had full confidence and self-reliance, she presented the paper nicely and was applauded.

After lunch the third session was rather small and she left for the hotel as she could not be intimate with anybody. A few postgraduate students and research scholars of H.P. University were taking care of arrangements and she felt a little bored. She ordered for coffee and snacks and rested in bed for a while. After 6.30 P.M. she left hotel to have a walk on the Mall Road. After fifteen minutes or so she came across Dr. Yamuna Kamal and greeted him (45). He was smartly dressed and recollected Yukti's face as seen in the conference. He smiled and said — 'Good evening Yukti. It was real pleasure to listen to your paper this noon. Really superb. You have aptitude for new thinking otherwise students these days don't study the history of revolution — its causes and effects. But you probably consulted the best authorities on the subject and could present a nice paper. Congratulations Yukti.'

'Thank you sir. You have perhaps spoken very high of me. Thanks again for blessings.' She mildly replied. And then requested him for a cup of coffee in nearby restaurant.

But he turned down her request and said — 'I am in a hurry as I wish to return to Ambala tonight. I haven't yet booked any hotel room and hence confused to stay here tonight or go back.' He said.

'But then — What is the hurry? There may be nice speakers tomorrow and you'll miss their lofty thoughts. Better stay! You can share the room with me if you deem fit.' Yukti suggested.

'But it'll be inconvenient to you that way.' He said with a little disinterestedness.

'Not at all sir. You are staying now. No confusion on this issue.'

Both of them moved towards the hotel Rivoli where she had stayed in room number 315. Dr. Yamuna Kamal enjoyed coffee and dry fruits as served by Yukti.

He asked her — 'What do you intend to do after passing M.A.?'

'Join research.'

'Fine, which field have you selected for research? Any particular author of your interest? Any particular age or Anglo-Indian author?' He asked with full curiosity.

'Not yet. I'm studying in M.A. (Pre.) at present. I'll seek your help when the time comes.'

'No problem. I am qualified to guide research scholars and so far produced three research scholars. But then you're supposed to work hard for high percentage of marks in M.A. Then you'll have to clear entrance test of the university to join research. And then course work of a year.'

'How long to work for a Ph.D.?'

'Nearly five years.'

'That's a pretty long time. My parents have started talking of my marriage. Only my mummy supports me for higher studies. Often I wish to join research in a foreign university. But then I'll have to pass M.A. from there. That way I grow old before I am a Ph.D.' She pined.

But smart Professor felt all this and as she was wearing a shoulderless blouse, he put his right hand on her shoulder and assured — 'Why to get that much worried? I may help you. Ph.D. is a Ph.D. whether you take from Indian University or from Oxford University. Why not join Kurukshetra University where I may get your dream fulfilled easily.'

'Really sir"' She asked with a glitter in her eyes.

'Yes. Really, you may trust me. If you are ready to study and work under my supervision, I can manage U.G.C. scholarship for you. At the same time you may prepare for N.E.T. too. I'll thoroughly guide you.'

'Thank you sir in advance.' She said.

Since Yukti had not removed his hand from her shoulder, he felt the signal and felt confirmed of her acceptance when she hugged him with her thanks-giving. After all, her dream project was going to get materialized and all of a sudden she had found a research supervisor in Ambala itself. Professor put his hand on her back and rubbed there. It was enough to excite a young girl who had not enjoyed amorous relations so far.

Yukti didn't speak a word when the Professor pressed her hips and passionately kissed her. She thought — Where did he survive earlier? Why had she not joined Arya College where research facilities were available and good library was open 24×7. She was fully excited with his shower of kisses and they moved towards the bed to make love.

Wise Yukti didn't think for a moment that she was being deflowered for research — the maximum price she was going to pay for her academic ambition. She forgot the promise that she had made with mummy and had sudden outburst of passion. Dr. Yamuna Kamal didn't feel it necessary to attend the conference next day and both of them enjoyed love-making without being aware of time. Yet she proposed to meet him soon in Ambala for further studies and then they left the room for Ambala.

Professor was not happy with his wife and prepared himself to love with Yukti. But it was beginning of passionate moments in Yukti's life. Since she got enough money from parents, she could hire a hotel for pleasant time with her new mentor. Yukti's passion for Prof. Yamuna Kamal didn't subside that soon as she was pretty smart and highly aspiring for her aim and her academic aim could be achieved with his help only. So, she decided not to discontinue this relationship at any cost. Now, Yukti accepted this friends-with-benefit relationship to fulfill her materialistic as well as academic desires with resources of professor.

28

Like the first rose of spring, Dipali was ever fresh and pretty. But she remained almost a recluse as she didn't talk on topics commonly discussed by other girls of 21st century. Of course, she played billiards, ping pong and tennis with girls who tried to win her favour. She took education to become a cultured and civilized lady though her parents had asked her to get married after passing B.A.

Her father Lala Sarang had worked as a builder in Greater Noida but returned to Panipat as he felt allured towards his agriculture farm of four hundred bighas. Here he observed his childhood friend Lala Narang earning money with blanket manufacturing and exports. Lala Sarang made a survey of the market and hired an M.B.A. to start export of carpets to African and Asian countries. He didn't take the risk of exports to Europe as it needed a lot of extra money.

On paper he was an exporter and manufacturer of blankets too. But then the unit of blankets was lying rusted. He used to import old woollen clothes from Europe as raw material for blankets. But most importantly, one of his assistant managers sold half of them to the readymade garment dealers. Many coats, jackets and pants were in good condition. Two drycleaners used to clean them with white petrol and then iron them. They were packed so well that they appeared to have been imported. This trick enhanced his profits. Lala Sarang took other clothes for recycling as thread and then woven as fabric.

Dipali left for Shimla by her own Honda City car along with her driver and guardian on Sunday. After attending the third session of world conference she returned to Evelyn Hotel and lunched. Then she returned to her hotel to complete the reading of the novel *Lady Chatterley's Lover* by D.H. Lawrence. Actually, *Women In Love* was prescribed in the fiction paper.

Since the college Professor referred to another novel too, she was reading it for fun sake. Here she had many questions in her mind such as 'Why did Lady Chatterley love her attendant Mellors? How could she not control her passion and obsession? Was British ethics loose in 20th century society? Why did she not bother for social values? Why did she not take divorce from her invalid husband? Did she really attach importance to his money, status and standard of living? Did she not cheat her husband that way?

However, she herself felt excited while reading the love adventures of Lady Chatterley and Mellors and failed to resist. Yet good sense prevailed in her. She danced with an unknown stranger in the Rock Music Room of the hotel and then dined. She gave him her fake cell number and returned to her room.

After three days Kamala Nain proposed her to visit Patiala as the former wanted to write an article on the monarchs of Punjab. Dipali's classmates Neeru had often talked of the grandeur of the palace of Patiala and hence they left for Patiala for fun. It was two days programme towards the end of November, 2019 and she felt excited.

Patiala's Palace of Raja Inderjeet Singh was grand in itself and due to Neeru they were permitted to enter the palace easily.

Here they observed the luxuries that Prince and the Queen enjoyed. There was a retinue of servants and guards and a Puja Sthal of silver where *Guruvani* had been put and the saint took care of it. Of course, they were asked at the gate to cover their head with Dupatta.

There was a feeling in the heart of Dipali — Had she become the princess of this palace, it would have been very fortunate. However, the P.A. to the young prince Inderjeet had taken notice of attractive Dipali and took her picture silently and secretly so as to show to the prince. The visitors to the palace were supposed to register their names, address and phone number at the entrance gate and he took her address and cell number from there.

Since birth Dipali was generally addressed with nick name Victoria as the Pandit had prophesied that she had the fate lines of Queen Victoria herself. Lala Sarang never expected that his daughter would be the wife of a monarch as days of monarchy had gone from India.

In the Maharaja Garden they all observed the large variety of flowers and beauty of large fountain. Statue of Cupid was installed in the middle of the fountain. Many tulips — White, red and yellow blossomed here and they took selfie again and again. They could see the view of grand building of Maharaja Medical College of Patiala from the Garden. Diapli had a desire to see the birth of a baby and the agonies that a lady felt at the time of delivery. Neeru had intimated the lady doctor for this and they were supposed to stand outside the operation theatre at 1 O' clock.

Dipali observed through the glass window — a pregnant lady was crying with labour pain. She was carried to the operation table and fluid was coming out of her vagina. The vagina was slowly and slowly opening its mouth and then the nurse asked the lady to push the child out and another nurse consoled the lady who was badly crying — 'All will be well soon. We are here to take care of you. Push and try to push further.'

Within two-three minutes the baby got delivered with head first and then whole body. His connecting link with the mother was cut and the nurse took him to clean. The lady got wonderful relief with the delivery and decided not to have another baby at any cost. After all, delivery of a baby is second birth of the mother.

As a matter of fact, Neeru was the eldest daughter of P.A. Surendra Singh and had created the interest of the Prince through her father in Dipali. So far the Prince took it lightly and didn't bother much.

Today the P.A. Surender Singh told Prince's mother, the Queen to have a look at Dipali as she had fortunately come to Patiala. The Queen agreed to meet Dipali and the three girls were asked to have lunch with the Queen and Prince Inderjeet Singh.

Just after seeing rosy Dipali, Prince Inderjeet Singh said to himself — 'She is pretty really — well built, blossomed flower, meant for a prince.'

So far Dipali had no idea that she was going to be interviewed for matrimonial purpose. Even without changing her dress, she shined as a full moon and the Queen felt interested in her. Queen asked her about her family members and the trade her father did. Still Dipali had no idea that she had won the heart of Prince Inderjeet Singh and tomorrow will be a new day in her life. But then Cupid had hit them both with his arrows.

It was just a matter of chance that Inderjeet Singh and Dipali could not talk to each other privately, alone by themselves. Queen was not in haste.

Kamala Nain enquired things about the royal family though much was available on the website. After lunch Dipali was gifted a gold wrist watch and her friends were gifted silk sarees. P.A. was asked to contact Lala Sarang if the latter had any objection to Dipali's marriage with Prince Inderjeet Singh.

Lala Sarang needed sometime to discuss the marriage issue with his worthy wife and daughter though he recollected the

T

R

U

T

H

F

U

L

prophecy of the astrologer.

The image of Inderjeet Singh appeared before the mental eyes of Dipali and then disappeared. She failed to keep the picture of her hero in her heart and felt sad with this physical limitation. Prince Inderjeet Singh wished to detain her in the palace after she had left. But then there were royal manners and he didn't dare to disobey the royal protocol.

But the eyes of Dipali looked towards the gold watch again and yet again but then the watch didn't utter a word. How sad! She felt that Queen paid attention to her figure and personality and noted that the young beauty looked towards Inderjeet Singh stealthily. But then Dipali was neither witty nor talkative and hence there was no long conversation between them.

Next day Sardar Surendra Singh made a phone call to Lala Sarang and informed him of his arrival there. That gave confirmed idea to Dipali and her parents that things were moving in the right direction. Prince as well as Dipali had started seeing dreams of marriage and then future generations of Patiala.

Lala Sarang asked her frankly — 'Do you really like Inderjeet?'

She kept silent.

He asked again — ' You're my only daughter. Since you have visited the castle of Prince and accepted gold watch from the Queen, that confirms that you accept him. But then this is the only time for final answer. Like him and love him or else dislike him and forget him. No other way out my Victoria!'

She nodded her head as acceptance and her mother confirmed — 'She is feeling shy like common girls. You may proceed further.'

Sardar Surender Singh presented eleven packets of sweets, eleven packets of dry fruits, one big basket of fruits, eleven sarees and three diamond sets for Dipali and asked Lala ji — 'I hope you have finalized the marriage issue of Dipali ji with Prince Inderjeet of Patiala.'

'Yes, I accept this proposal in the name of God.'

Finally, he took lunch there and was almost forced to accept a male shawl for himself as a gift from Lala Sarang.

From the point of security of royal people, Mehndi, ring-ceremony, garlanding and seven rounds of fire were arranged in the large garden attached with the palace of Maharaja.

Shopping was done by Dipali to her heart's content and a lot of gold and diamond relics were offered to her by the Queen.

In the circle of her classmates, Naini, Kamala Nain, Neeru and I attended her wedding and were gifted jeans and jackets by the Queen. As princess, she really became Victoria and recollected her childhood when parents addressed her as Victoria. Queen also addressed her Victoria of Patiala.

After three days of marriage celebration, the couple left for Switzerland for their honeymoon.

After two weeks of honeymoon, Dipali was ordered by the Queen to take care of Maharaja Hospital, three spinning mills and cultivation of more than three thousand bighas of land. She had all possible comforts of a royal life and Inderjeet Singh had asked all the staff members to address her as Queen Victoria II.

❐

29

The general mistake committed by human beings is that they mostly listen half-truth, understand a quarter but tell others double. And the result is moral debauchery and birth of misunderstanding.

Since I had studied fifteen essays of Francis Bacon on practical wisdom, I knew how to overcome half-truth and escape from its disastrous consequences. In spite of the result of my keen passion for madam I had decided firmly to face the oddities of life come what may.

Tomorrow was expected to be a free day as Mr. Singhal and his assistant were supposed to look into business. I had started listening to youtube lectures on books prescribed for M.A. (Pre.) English feeling — Nobody knows when luck comes. I ought to be ready to

W
E
L
C
O
M
E

it.

But then madam got a call on her phone that fifteen New Jersey cows had arrived on the farm and she was supposed to pay forty-five lac rupees for them. In addition to this she was to pay two lac rupees for squeezing machines so that milk may be taken out automatically from the udders. Naturally madam asked me to get ready immediately and within half an hour we were on the farm.

One supervisor had been sent by the director of I.V.R.I Haryana to train our man and look after the sensitive cows. Due to her busy schedule she could not get the tin shade prepared for them and hence the contractor was asked to follow the instructions of the supervisor. Money was paid by cheque and then the supervisor left after having tea with us in the farmhouse.

It was no problem to find out another caretaker for the cows. Within two days the tin shade was to be readied and urban milk vendors were ready to buy milk in bulk. Fifty bighas of land was prepared as a barn for them and one bull was kept purposely on the farm. After all, madam was not prepared to forget the idea of procreation.

Now each orphan of Ambala town was to get 250 gram milk per person and three litter was enough for us. Necessary porridge was purchased and the farm was fully electrified for safety purpose. Everything was to be kept neat and clean and timing was very important. It was the beginning of dairy business and she decided to visit the farm on alternate days.

In the scorching heat of the sun we reached the bungalow, relaxed a little and planned for dairy management. Whatever, she had studied in the book on dairy management, was implemented fully. To make her smile I passed the remark — 'Their udders are bigger than those of Mrs. Slipslop.'

'Really? You saw only the udders and not the whole body of cows — how healthy they are.'

'Yes. You are right. I hope this is your dream project darling.'

'Of course, why to think of their udders when I am here to embrace you.'

And she embraced me passionately and we made love before lunch. After lunch she told me — 'You'll get better milk to drink twice a day. Secondly, never forget taking almonds and big raisins regularly. Is it O.K.?'

'Yes. O.K.'

That evening weather was a little dusty and slow winds were blowing. After dinner we watched T.V. for some time and then entered the bed. But the weather had been constantly changing, As we were inside the bed, we heard a lot of lightning and thundering and the sound of torrent rains.

Madam came closer to me saying — 'This thundering reminds me of tornado of Uttarakhand in 2013 which killed a lot of people. Many villagers became homeless and jobless.'

'Yes. Don't get worried and try to sleep.'

We had a disturbed sleep as we felt there was something wrong on the roof top at this time. The regular electric supply had stopped and the generator supplemented it.

But the guard saw many large cracks in the walls of the bungalow in the morning and rang the bell. As we reached the elevator, we found it was not working. Yet we got down the stairs and came out to confirm what he had said. We felt shocked seeing several cracks on all the four walls though the bungalow was nearly thirty five years old.

She made a phone call to the contractor to reach there soon. After observing the creaks he told her — 'There is not much to worry for. They can be repaired. But let us go at the top of second floor and have a look at the roof there.'

Yet the elevator didn't work. We were badly sad to see that the whole lintel had very large and big gaps apart from minor cracks. The contractor immediately told madam — 'Sorry, madam, the whole lintel has got to be constructed again. Last night lightning has damaged it badly.'

Madam really felt sad at heart. So far both of us had talked of the bright side of nature but this dark night made us conscious of its dark moods. Men are really helpless when nature is angry with them. Without expressing her intense grief she asked him to do the needful.

From the newspapers we came to know that thunder and lightning had created panic in Ambala and the surrounding areas. News was pitiable and all residents found themselves helpless.

Chanchal told madam that the freeze was out of order. Then I noticed that T.V. too was not functioning. Two computers were damaged by lightning. There was some or other defect in electric wiring and we decided to have new electric fitting with opening wires. It was a pathetic scene inside home. This is how Nature had shown her wrath towards people.

The contractor had left after giving solace and consolation to both of us but unfortunate event had happened and Madam was badly desperate. In bed I tried to take her in my arms but she was unwilling to cooperate.

She told me with tears in her eyes — 'What will happen if another tornado turns this bungalow into desert. I have seen many ruined castles in Rajasthan, Karnataka and Maharashtra. Probably we all will be lying crushed under the debris crying like my paralyzed mother. No, Pritesh, no. I am not prepared to lead the life of a paralyzed widow like my mother. My expected son will die before coming to this world. Unbearable. Really horrible sight to seek help and cry in the wilderness. All this pomp and show will vanish with another lightning, another thunder will make us homeless. Didn't you see gaps in the lintel of the roof? How could I help if walls had fallen down! Perhaps this house is no more safe for us.'

I told her — 'Don't stretch the probabilities too far lest the wires should break. The worst is over and the whole bungalow is not made of mere sand. Try to control yourself if you have negative psychology.'

I knew that she won't be ready for romance at this time as her anguish was pretty deep and keen.

Just then I got a call from Kammo — 'Bhai, please help me as I am reaching your bungalow any minute. I am being chased by the police as the latter wish to take revenge from us.' And she switched off the phone.

Within next three minutes I tried to analyze the character of Kammo and Shanu and of course Toshi — 'What the hell these two girls have done? Why is police chasing them at this late hour? How can I help them against the wishes of madam? If they are criminals, let them suffer?'

But then the call bell rang and I came down to open the door for Kammo. Shanu was with her. As I opened the door, two bullets were fired at Kammo and Shanu and both of them fell down dead in no time. Ladhu was third man to come out of car and the third bullet killed him.

Next day's newspaper narrated their crimes and gave a message — 'As you sow, so shall you reap.'

◻

30

That day proved to be saddest for us as two sub-inspectors of police visited us twice asserting — 'Look Pritesh, this is a criminal case. Either you reveal your relation with three criminals or we adopt our means to make you speak?' His tone was rough and tough.

I replied humbly — 'I don't know these three fellows at all. Secondly, I hate such rascals who take law in their hands.'

'But the question arises'.

'Why did Kammo ring you up?' He asked further.

'I can't reply that. If I recollect I met her in the marriage ceremony of my younger brother and that is all.'

'How could she have your cell number? How could she depend upon your support?'

'Sir. I can't reply this. Since I belong to Panipat, Kammo might have known my cell number from there.'

'Mr. Pritesh you are hiding facts from us.'

'Not at all. Sir. I'll positively help you if I come to know anything related to this.' I assured him with folded hands. After seeing the pictures of my late father-in-law and late captain Vinamra he said — 'You probably belong to the family of Defence people. Don't move out of the town for a week. When you go out, please inform us.' He took my cell phone and then departed.

'O.K. Sir.'

Madam contacted Sarpanch and requested him to do the needful. But one sub-inspector took it otherwise and asked Sarpanch — 'If Pritesh has not done anything, why has he sent you to plead in his defence?'

'Well, the couple is afraid of police authorities. Moreover, the criminals are dead and many secrets lie buried with their dead bodies. Is it not a deterrent punishment?'

'O.K. I'll see to it. But then Pritesh is to be doubted.'

Madam and I felt restlessness though Sarpanch told her that needful has been done and the police authorities won't trouble you. L.I.U. reports of Karnal Police Station will be really useful to them. The P.A. of Ladhu has been arrested along with the night guard of farmhouse. Let us see how the wind blows?'

And then he left.

In the evening we offered prayers to Lord Shiva and Lord Krishna earnestly and needed their moral support.

That night madam cried in sleep as she felt the agonies of Queen Isabella who had amorous relations with Younger Mortimer. She was Isabella and was being punished for cooperating with younger Mortimer against Edward II. Her son Edward III had a sword in his hand and loudly sought revenge — 'You faithless mother! Why did you plan the murder of my father Edward II? Your sin can't be pardoned at any cost.'

As he raised his sword to kill her, madam cried loudly — 'No. My dear son. These courtiers are against my husband. I am no bitch to kill my worthy husband. Trust me.'

I had not yet slept due to the rough conduct of police inspector and felt sad when madam cried out of grief.'

'No, no my son. If at all you doubt my role in the scandal, please forgive your innocent mother.'

But she had my hand in her hand and had embraced me for security. I found her a patient of neurosis and yet tried to give relief to her. I told her — 'There is nobody to kill you. Please come out of your dream.'

She took a few minutes to feel a little normal and was badly sweating. With the towel lying nearby I wiped her body and asked her to feel bold and brave. After she had checked her pistol under the pillow, she felt at ease. But I felt really upset with her tragic dreams and failed to understand — Why does she see only horrible dreams.'

Next night was further troublesome for both of us as Madam felt herself to be Desdemona and observed Othello ready to kill her due to his jealousy.

In the dream Othello asked her to produce the handkerchief that he had given her. He blamed her for presenting the same to Cassio and asked 'Why did you flirt with Lt. Cassio? You wanton woman! You have disgraced my marriage bed! You slut, you have no right to survive due to faithlessness.'

'But you are mistaken my lord!'

'I'm not wanton as I have been sincere and faithful to my dear husband.' She cried.

'It is not suitable for you to make use of words like sincere and faithful. Had you been sincere, you won't have played with my emotions.'

As Othello raised his sword to kill her she cried — 'Please don't punish your Desdemona. It'll be a bad precedent for generations.'

I heard her words 'a bad precedent for generations' and asked her to come to reality.

'Please madam, there is nobody here. Forget the impressions of dream and come to reality.'

Then she cried — 'Oh, My God! What the hell! Othello has killed my spirit.' And wept a lot.

I decided to take her to a Psychiatrist for the treatment of her dreams and to know the reasons for her dullness and anguish. Within last two weeks she had lost cheerfulness of her face. The killing of Kammo, Shanu and Ladhu further added to her sorrow as she told me — 'Three more deaths at the gate of our bungalow. These rascals chose my house for death. I had enough memories of death in my mind.'

Madam had picture of small babies in bedroom and drawing room so that she may think of bright side of pregnancy and may deliver nice babies. Her gynecologist Dr. Nanda had told me that she is conceiving twins. It was not to be worried about as nobody can guide and control the working of Nature and Fate. We were planning the names to be given to our twins. A lot of toys and clothes were bought for them. But that joy evaporated due to her regular dreams and their permanent impressions had settled in her unconscious mind.

I tried my best to create her interest in trading of shawls and blankets. Then I discussed the project of cows. I told her that sugarcane crop has been quite profitable and seeds have been sown for wheat crops. Wheat crop was expected to be quite profitable. But alas! She left all interest in the construction of orphanage and village school.

As the assembly elections had been declared Sarpanch met us on the farm and expressed his desire to contest the election for legislative assembly. Because his house was rather small, he needed the farmhouse for three weeks and then requested madam for a car for two months. Madam asked him to borrow a car on hire and promised to pay half cost of hiring and petrol. She was not willing to handover the farmhouse to him for three weeks but had to adjust as Sarpanch had always helped her through thick and thin.

The psychiatrist Dr. Nanda asked me to take care of her round the clock and suggested —

- Don't discuss any serious problems with her.
- Let her lead a carefree life.
- Don't quarrel with her on any issue.
- Make love to her sincerely.
- Let her eat the food that she likes.
- Be positive in life. Let her be positive towards future.
- Create hopes in her.
- Remove all literature full of violence, murder and dark thoughts from bedroom.
- Let her avoid financial problems if any.
- Enjoy outing as and when possible.
- Let her enjoy the beauty of flowers.
- Let her enjoy music of her liking.

I felt as if I got a full time job to help her come out of her neurosis. I knew for sure — the results would be disastrous if she is not looked after. I took care of the hostel, harvesting, milk business, construction of bank building, building, trading etc. Chanchal and Dhania were asked to be extra conscious of her food. Often she aspired to play billiards with me and I took her to that room and played. She found some relief as she was almost asleep for eighteen hours due to Alprax 1 mg. and Quitpin 25 mg.

Since my younger sister and brother had their examination, I could not invite my mummy for help. I became almost on attendant for my sick wife. But then misfortunes come in bulk and don't wither away that easily.

After two nights she saw a dream and presumed herself to be Duchess of Malfi. Since she loved Antonio, a man of inferior rank, her two brothers Ferdinand and Cardinal didn't approve her remarriage with him. Bosola created unfavourable situation for her one after another. Being separated from Antonio and feeling fed up with the rough treatment of brothers, she cried —

'Kill me. And bring down heaven upon me. At least you should have a peaceful sleep.' And she cried loudly — 'a peaceful sleep' and wept a lot.

I could understand that she had seen another terrible dream to make her cry. I requested her to come to senses and feel normal.

'You are already asleep madam!'

'No. My brothers want to kill me as they can't tolerate my remarriage.'

'But then you have no brothers.'

'Oh, my God! Yes, I have no brothers. How foolish of me to imagine dream-brothers'.

She felt normal after five-six minutes and embraced me. But then I felt that she perhaps needed another psychiatrist from Delhi. As Dr. Nanda was informal with me, he visited our bungalow that evening. After coffee I invited him to play badminton and that he relished very much. As I told him about our table of billiards, he accompanied me there and enjoyed a game as a fresher.

Before he left he met madam and told her — 'Take life easy. Don't have unnecessary tensions. If you continue to cry in dreams, you'll have to take more sleeping pills. Much depends upon your bent of mind. Do remember that too much consumption of pills will harm your babies.'

When I gifted him a shawl for his wife, he replied — 'But I don't have a wife to use it. I am a divorcee.'

'Why did a woman take divorce from a loving person like you?' I politely asked.

'Perhaps it was fated. Local lady Dr. Santoshi Nanda is my ex-wife. She said- 'If I don't dominate, I will be dominated.' So, I took divorce as she was too assertive. I hate to be ordered — do this, don't do that. Now both of us are free nightingales flying freely in the horizon. No restrictions.'

And he left.

I continued to lead a thoughtful life and yet managed time to love madam. Often I noticed the amorous eyes of Chanchal observing my activities but then I ignored her totally and regarded her worthless.'

The journey of life continued in this bungalow. After three weeks Sarpanch met me with the keys of farmhouse saying that he failed to get the party ticket. The man, who had promised him ticket, demanded twenty lacs when ticket is handed over to him. Prudent as Sarpanch was, he actually depended upon thirty bighas of land that his father had left him. He told me that he would never contest any election as the cost and result of election are uncertain.

As expected, madam delivered two sons in June with caesarian operation. Still both of us were happy as we expected joy in the bungalow. We had planned to give them names Shree and Raj Shree. To our horror the babies had jaundice, a disease that normally catches small kids. What can't be cured must be endured! There were wrinkles of sorrow on her face as kids had to be separated in I.C.U. and the Child Specialist took care of them. For two days and two nights, their condition was static but third day doctor warned me — 'Any damn thing may happen as kids are not responding to medicines. God only knows what will happen next.'

I didn't dare to reveal this to madam and analyzed the bad results if I get sad news. And the same happened at 5 P.M. Now I had no option but to tell madam that we are unfortunate parents to have missed our lovely kids. She cried a lot and it was hell of a problem to control her agonies. I felt non-plussed though Dhania and Chanchal were with me.

Madam could not be discharged from maternity ward as her stitches were fresh. The nurses put their dead bodies in my car. Madam instructed me not to bury them in the funeral ground where other children were normally buried. She told me to bury them in the compound of our bungalow from where she could see their graves. At least dead children have their share in our land.

Following her advice I returned to the bungalow and asked the gardener and his son to dig two graves for our sons who had actually only three days' life at their disposal. I had no other thought in my mind except that the bungalow had witnessed two more dead bodies, to be lamented forever.

After their calm burial I took bath and reached the hospital to be with madam. She had no sleep as grief had captured her strongly. Since I was silent, she asked — 'Have you buried them?'

'Yes.'

'What else did you do?'

'I just recited the Gayatri Mantra and requested Lord Shiva to grant peace to their soul.'

'I told you earlier that nobody can predict the working of KAAL and the same proved true today. They were not fated to add joy to our life and hence left.'

'Yes. Kaal does not care for the agonies of survivors.' I told her.

After another three days Madam was discharged from the hospital and reached bungalow. Dhania helped her taking bath. She put on salwar kameez and offered prayers to Lord. She wanted to see the business affairs. But she accepted my request to stay in bedroom for two days more. Since I had been upset for the last six days, she asked — 'What makes you so restless?'

'Nothing in particular. But then realities can't be forgotten that easily.'

'Yes. But Pritesh, life can't be led with mere negative emotions. Since babies must have forgotten our faces, we must forget them. Come on and be cheerful. Life does not end with their departure. Come closer to me as I wish to assure you of my love for you darling. Let us make a new beginning young as we are. God willing, all will be well next time and this house does not have any curse of barrenness.'

She kissed me passionately and then laughed loudly and said — 'Welcome each rebuff that turns earth's smoothness rough ...'

She added after full self-cleaning — 'Let us dance, sing, play games, meet friends, enjoy the beauty of seasons and listen the songs of cuckoo and nightingales and eat fruits of our liking. Forget the past and plan for new tomorrow and welcome new tomorrow. We haven't lost interest in question-answer in K.B.C. of life. And she laughed again to regain her interest in life. To my mind it was the result of her self-illumination and auto-suggestion.

.

CPSIA information can be obtained
at www.ICGtesting.com
Printed in the USA
BVHW061718310323
661545BV00016B/116

9 789356 842588